Sorority of the Ninth Fold

Sorority of the Ninth Fold

PETER HACKIEWICZ

To Marie my sister-in-law.
May the creator's breath keep those pricy wings of yours aloft until our family reunites in our Father's house. You are deeply missed.

❯ PREFACE ❮

I wanted to share three quotes from one of my favorite books, *A Christmas Carol* by Charles Dickens.

"They are Man's and they cling to me, appealing from their fathers. This boy is ignorance and this girl is Want. Beware them both, and all of their degree, but most of all beware this boy for on his brow I see that written which is Doom, unless the writing be erased." Charles Dickens, *A Christmas Carol*

"There are some upon this earth of yours who lay claim to know us, and who do their deeds of passion, pride, ill-will, hatred, envy ,bigotry, and selfishness in our name; who are as strange to us and all our kith and kin, as if they had never lived. Remember that, and charge their doing on themselves not us." Charles Dickens, *A Christmas Carol*

"Men's courses will foreshadow certain ends, to which, if preserved in, they must lead," said Scrooge. "But if the courses be departed from, the ends will change." Charles Dickens, *A Christmas Carol*

Sorority of the Ninth Fold

One

⇻ BURIAL GROUNDS ⇺

*Then I saw a new heaven and a new Earth, for the old heaven and
the old Earth had disappeared. And the sea was also gone. Rev 21*

It was that typical humid Midwestern summer morning: you
get out of the shower and you feel as though you need a
shower. I laid out three graves and passed them along to the
digging crew, but the real drama would be because of the inbound funerals. Seven gravesides and eight chapels: not too bad.
But with vacations and an aging staff the services will be a
challenge. The biggest challenge for me right now though was
working clear headed without adequate sleep.

This damn recurring dream I have been having. Couple times
a night it's got me spooked. Bits and pieces of the dream stuck
in my head, plaguing my daytime thoughts, causing catatonic
stares, turning deeply buried memories to daydreams. There is
this attractive red headed woman, I get the impression she is a
witch, she wants me to do something for her and she is using
her feminine wiles to get my attention. Well, she got my attention to a point of psychosis. I had my paperwork sorted on the

dash and I was on point waiting for the first funeral so I could lead it to the graveside so the bereaved can have their committal service. Then on my lead sheet I saw the back was no longer blank. By the look of the handwriting, I wrote it, but I don't remember writing it.

> *Late evening Sun paints with hues of*
> *Lavender and Rose.*
> *Rush of lilac wind jars the French doors*
> *Sensuously sculpted woman of purest*
> *Ivory Tusk,*
> *Draped in silk and lace Wisps of fiery hair flicker-crackle*
> *My hand paws my chest as if*
> *To tear the flesh above my*
> *Heart; An embrace without a kiss?*
> *Holding a pillow of daydreamt memories*
> *As if they were you.*

I looked up to see a white van with government plates just whiz by; as soon as I went to pursue it slowed down and pulled to the curb. Two army soldiers got out of the van, one male one female. The woman was on the short side and stood in front of me. I didn't have my clipboard. I simply held the list and asked, "What is the name of the deceased and or church and or funeral director?" The male soldier reaching inside his pocket retrieved his informational piece of paper. They both seemed so young, or I was just getting old.

"Yes sir, it is an eleven-fifteen arrival for Strauss funeral home. They called this morning. They were running short of honor guards and we were dispatched from the base." The young soldier's voice was sharp and respectful. The unseen thing of the scene was that the female soldier was reading the back of the lead sheet. It was right at eye level for her; she couldn't help it.

The young female soldier felt like half her brain just got slapped, the rousing out of bed early this morning to go to a cemetery, to be

2

on honor guard duty. Several weeks ago she joined a secret society called 'The Sorority of the Ninth Fold.' She joined because she knows deep inside this Troyon alliance is just a bad deal. She was given a metal tag with numbers on it and she was told, "You must give this tag to a love struck man!" They were told their missions may be strange but, for secrecy's sake, they had to do them without question. They were also to be as covert as possible.

The cemetarian's hands pointed as he explained, "I will lead the funeral down this road, when yours comes in be parked on the side and I will wave you in the procession."

"That does not work for us sir! We have a flag folding ceremony that we need to set up," the young soldier explained. The cemetery man's fingers ground into his furrowed brow, thinking of a settlement that would meet all needs.

"What kind of set up are we talking here?" the cemetarian asked.

"We have a podium in the van with a small speaker and mike. The funeral director will recite the procedure as we fold the flag," the male soldier explained.

"Okay then back in your van, follow me. When I stop, you stop in back of me. You must leave your van there. I will pull the hearse to back of your van, so follow me and stay where I leave you so you are not in the way," the cemetarian explained.

"Roger that," the soldier replied. The cemetarian reached out his hand and shook the soldier's hand and said, "Thank you for your service."

As he turned to shake the hand of the woman soldier, she reached her hand out saying "You are familiar to me; we must have friends in common." He felt the metal as he shook her hand and said nothing; their eyes met briefly, exchanging volumes of emotion in soulful conversation. He was getting into his truck perplexed on what just happened, as if his brain had skipped a beat of time. He slid the tag into his cargo pocket and drove to the proper graveside location. "What the hell is going on?" his sleep deprived brain shouted.

Now, between the outside traffic delays, going long or short for mass and people running late and extended memorial services, Strauss was the last inbound and the lead man's responsibility to service. He parked the funeral. Getting back to the hearse he pointed to the funeral director at his head signaling to bring the casket on a head first set up. The director called his pall bearers and explained to face outward and carry the casket following the cemetarian. The honor guard slowly saluted the casket draped in its American flag pall. The grounds man grabbed a hold and helped set it on the lowering device.

He never even peeked at that piece of metal in his pocket, didn't know if he wanted to, just wanted to do what he was supposed to and he didn't know yet what that was. He moved off to the side, as the funeral director went to the podium and the honor guard took hold of the flag. He was sweating like crazy and it always impressed him how these soldiers always wore such heavy clothes and never passed out. There was a slight electronic buzz as the funeral director turned the mike on. He held a laminated sheet with the flag folding ceremony written on it, and the funeral director began to speak. "A properly proportioned flag will fold thirteen times on the triangles, representing the thirteen Original Colonies. When finally complete the triangular folded flag is emblematical of the tri-corner hat worn by the Patriots of the American Revolution. When folded, no red or white stripe is to be evident, leaving only the honor field of blue and stars. The flag folding ceremony represents the same religious principles on which our country was originally founded. The portion of the flag denoting honor is the canton of blue containing the stars representing the states our veterans served in uniform. The canton field of blue dresses from left to right and is inverted when draped as a pall on a casket of a veteran who has served our country in uniform.

In the Armed Forces of the United States, at the ceremony of retreat the flag is lowered, folded in a triangle and kept under watch throughout the night as a tribute to our nation's honored dead. The next morning it is brought out and, at the ceremony of reveille, run aloft as a symbol of our belief in the resurrection of the body." The honor guards were removing the flag from the funeral pyre, like they were acting in a small narrated play.

"The first fold of our flag is a symbol of life.

The second fold is a symbol of our belief in the eternal life.

The third fold is made in honor and remembrance of the veteran departing our ranks who gave a portion of life for the defense of our country to attain a peace throughout the world.

The fourth fold represents our weaker nature, for as American citizens trusting in God, it is to Him we turn in times of peace as well as in times of war for His divine guidance.

The fifth fold is a tribute to our country, for in the words of Stephen Decatur, 'Our country, in dealing with other countries, may she always be right; but it is still our country, right or wrong.'

The sixth fold is for where our hearts lie. It is with our heart that we pledge allegiance to the flag of the United States of America, and to the republic for which it stands, one nation under God, indivisible, with liberty and justice for all.

The seventh fold is a tribute to our Armed Forces, for it is through the Armed Forces that we protect our country and our flag against all her enemies, whether they're found within or outside of the boundaries of our republic.

The eighth fold is a tribute to the one who entered into the valley of the shadow of death, that we might see the light of day, and to honor Mother, for whom it flies on Mother's Day."

The honor guard very deliberately manipulated the flag, folding it as he spoke. A flock of about twenty noisy monk parrots filled a crab apple tree close by, with a momentary distraction of squawks and green commotion as they hurried away as randomly as they landed.

"The ninth fold is a tribute to womanhood; for it has been through their faith, love, loyalty and devotion that the characters of the men and women who have made this country great have been molded." The female solider felt a rush of three-fold pride fill her heart as the words were read.

"The tenth fold is a tribute to father, for he, too, has given his sons and daughters for the defense of our country.

The eleventh fold, in the eyes of a Hebrew citizen, represents the lower portion of the seal of King David and King Solomon, and glorifies, in their eyes, the God of Abraham, Isaac, and Jacob.

The twelfth fold, in the eyes of a Christian citizen, represents an emblem of eternity and glorifies, in their eyes, God the Father, the Son, and Holy Ghost. When the flag is completely folded, the stars are uppermost, reminding us of our national motto, 'In God we Trust.' After the flag is completely folded and tucked in, it takes on the appearance of a cocked hat, ever reminding us of the soldiers who served under General George Washington and the sailors and marines who served under Captain John Paul Jones who were followed by their comrades and shipmates in the Armed Forces of the United States, pre-serving for us the rights, privileges, and freedoms we enjoy today." The honor guard presented the flag to the widow, and marched away. The crane truck rolled up, my co-workers had come to tuck another one in for a long sleep.

Walking over to the truck I was greeted by Dan's voice. "Hey, they have been trying to get you on the radio Syl. Orders in the office to lay out. Go ahead, we got this." 'Animal pulled up in the screening truck, bases were covered so I left, but as I did I saw in the distance that solider. She had taken off her cover. She was a ginger girl. It was all tucked up with a black cloth covering her hair.

The metal in my pocket bit my thigh like a yellow jacket. Skulking to the office I did not want to interact with anyone so I basically reached around the corner and grabbed the orders out of their slot. I drove and parked by the dump site, the week's piles un-leveled. A pair of resident crows picked around for tidbits. These were the first pair Sylvester had seen back since the West Nile virus. Sylvester tossed the orders on the dash and finally pulled the metal tag from his pocket. It was a metal location tag with the lot, block and grave number of an interment, but it was in a small parish cemetery, St. Patrick's. Syl figured he would need a hand from an angel on this quest and a favor from his friend Dimitri the stone cutter.

Two

❧ THE CHASE ❦

"Nevertheless we, according to his promise look for a new heaven and a new Earth where in dwelleth righteousness."—2 Peter 3-13

Horses' hoofs punched the dampened dirt. They reared and sidestepped, their eyes bulging in their unholy quest. Misty rain mixed with lathering reins.

"Dismount!!" Captain Thorn ordered. "These witches have taken to the woods." He pointed to the matted fresh wet tracks that led into the tree line and motioned for his troops to make chase. His troop stood there as he dismounted. He drew his sword. "Forward!" he ordered waving his blade. The troop drew sword from sheath and advanced into the woodlands.

Brea's breath was hurried and noisy. "Hu Hu!!" She ran chaotically through the woods. She heard the chopping of the pursuing hunters, her mind was on fire and frantic. Heavily eroded soil around an old tethered tree showed a mass of roots, she twisted herself betwixt the exposed roots. She pulled her cloak up against herself. Her wrap acted like a chameleon skin. She took long large deep breaths and grabbed the amulet that

9

hung round her neck, her nose stung, her cheeks wet. She pushed it against her cleavage, feeling the hardness of the amethyst through the subtle smooth silk. Brea received the talisman from her father before he was killed, after escaping here from the future. Being accused of being a warlock shortly afterward, he was executed. "Use only in the direst emergency for it will have a crucial consequence," Brea's father told her the night before he was taken and sent the three girls in an opposite direction. A crackling blue outline seemed to sizzle around everything, pulsing white. Brea's astral adventure became her extraction mission.

She stood in the front room of a large suburban house. Walls looked iridescent white with a blue undertone, looking out the picture window down the subdivision of similar houses. This was freakishly familiar. A squad of soldiers marched down the center line of the street. Brea instinctively drew back against the wall as she breathed a hollow gasp. She heard a soft chuckle. "Can't see us, we're invisible, huh." The male figure stood there, he looked translucent. He rubbed his hands together as if it were cold.

"What magic is this sorcerer?" she questioned as her hand slowly slid to her belt, feeling for her wand.

"Dark matter magic," the ghostly sorcerer stated. "Your wand is not on this plane. Hell, I'm not entirely on this plane." His light laughs echoing in the air almost becoming sinister. "I'm your father's friend." His head turned back and forth, eyes straining. "Come closer Breezily. I can hardly see you." He reached out palms up. "Breezily", his voice hit her like a ton of bricks.

"Pete Renaissance!" she exclaimed walking toward him. Brea got close and her arms went through him giving her the chills—standing all her hair on end. "Sorry, just an apparition here, you are mostly ghostly to me. Your dad designed this portal corridor, he did a lot of his own work here. Hope it helps you find your solace, and your way home. Take the two spiders you find and put them to your ear. Listen to what they have to say and follow their instructions. I am running out of power to stay."

"I thought I lost you all. Once dad was killed we got caught up in just surviving," Brea began to explain as his apparition quickly faded.

Brea's conscience was struck hard, was her mind just allowing an escape route from reality to cope with the instability of the situation? She asked for help. She looked around the room and saw nothing. She heard marching approaching. This time it seemed more ominous. Two pale spiders were spinning down quickly from the ceiling, the silk almost invisible. "Naomi! Scarlet?" she thought." "What of my sisters?" She walked toward the spiders. Brea swiped the dark red hair around her ears, she felt the tapping of the spider's legs on her lobes. Brea's alabaster skin blended with the spider's pasty color.

"Separate the twisted silk." The one spider whispered as the other stroked Brea behind her ear, striving to comfort her. Brea walked around the silk they had just spun down on together. From one side a wee light glinted against the silk. A slight bulge separated the silk.

"Use your fingers and open the slat," the one spider explained. It was a low light passage, which had that same white outline-bent time bulge. Her palms could not remember the time they had touched such softness. She stepped inside and as she passed the entrance the spiders made haste and closed it. The spiders jumped back on her and mingled; becoming one spider and perching itself on her skull in back of her ear, then embedding itself in the skull behind the ear, physically incorporating itself into her hypothalamus.

Uncle Pete, Pete Renaissance who was coordinator for DARPA, used himself to test human enhancements so they would be able to survive the occupation. His other two brothers worked on projects but the information shared was filtered and they kept their distance as a security precaution. The spider communication network was working. Then there was the Imp

Nano. It started as a camouflage Nano covering the body and objects bending light and sound to avoid detection. Pete got loony, it seemed his internal enhancement constructed more synapses so he could do dark matter physics. His spider interfaced with his Imp Nano, which opened up a new realm of stealth, the Interdimensional Modular Platform (IMP). Once the subject was covered with the Imp Nanos they would release a minute dark energy pulse shifting the subject out of the present time. But what was discovered from that was even more interesting; a slit in the wallpaper of time, so to speak. During the pulse one could slide into the crease. Once the pulse stopped it would close behind you. Your spider could open it anywhere in the physical world and it was found that each person had their own, yet only one person at a time was able to go inside his or her own crevice, the spiders being the locking mechanism of that person's hideout. The door behind you shut and the Nanos helped you construct creature comforts in your new environment. The room seemed to construct itself to Brea thoughts.

The more she looked and engaged with her hideaway the more focused it became. The feel of the White Oak Bedroom dresser as a morning light seemed to emit itself from the round mirror. One side of the bureau had a silhouette head adorned on it was a witch's halo, the customary silver and gold wire in a crisscross pattern containing emeralds, diamonds, and amethyst quartz, woven throughout with the witch's own hair. Brea fondled the halo, marveling at its workmanship. Brea thought. "What's the harm? I'm not sitting on a loath stone." She placed the halo on her head.

Brea's dark red hair lightened to a fiery red as she adorned herself with a silver and gold web banded halo. The only green that outshone the emeralds were her green eyes.

The halo helps align the aura of its wearer through Charta's enhancing that tunes in the universe. (As Mother Earth, she would sit on the loath stone like the one in Scotland. This would be the throne of the Queen of Earth, Mother Nature's physical surrogate.)

As she stared into the looking glass she saw a large bedroom window with the sun rising behind her giving sun to the room, yet the physics of the corridor allowed no light to come from a window but light shone through the mirror, sunlight so warming and bright. As she looked into the mirror she saw someone approaching from its interior. Brea saw someone sitting in her reflected room. "Aster?" Brea questioned.

"Yes, I am Aster, you called to me," she said stoically. "You will have time to sleep, but you must first weigh your dreams of hope with the dreams of despair."

"Aster, help me." Brea's eyes were leaking tears; burning. "I need time to rest. This has all drained me so," she said in a delirious fit. The queen-size bed had four posts, representing the four Earthen elements and four of the woods, Pecan, Walnut, White Oak, Birch. She pulled down on the witch's halo and scurried to bed before her body gave out.

"Distance darkness fade away, I seek the mystic traveling ray. Reveal before my mind's bright eye the secrets I wish to spy." Brea repeated the phrase over and over she had accessed Aster's Grimoire. Brea had the luxury of mourning man's fate. She saw that is was necessary to act and in this sojourn she would find solace and emerge to take on man's attackers. Brea immersed herself in magick and incantation. Deep in that stillness within her she found that storehouse of universal knowledge. At that point her sojourn manifested itself to a green area by an expressway clover leaf in an outlying area of Chicago.

Brea woke in a bed covered in blood and sweat; the pillow soaked and smelled of vomit. 'I hoped to realize I was living someone else's nightmare. Whatever the situation the pervasive feeling of foreboding and loathing was totally overwhelming. My mind backtracks to Joshua, my father; I fear his cure may be as deadly as the Troyon scourge, but at least now it's our decision. Visions of a field of corpses grossly mutilated a true look at a collage of indignities, the fields of women's bodies after they have given birth to their plagued Troyon offspring.' Brea later entered in her journal.

Brea in her dream history saw the self-experimentation that transformed Uncle Pete's brain into a super synapsed augmented one after his self-inflicted experiments from brain boosting to Nano replication and structural reconfiguration. The days of wraith and rage when he released the Nano-factories and spiders into the environment to counter the Troyon attack. The spider's original job was communication, it would only transmit on a very narrow band once it linked with a web relay or hold the message for a later time when it would be undetected. They also incorporated filters that would filter out thoughts of people they really didn't want to be public. They also had a sliver of artificial intelligence that would prove invaluable as time went on. The entire system evolved by itself, the network became man's best friend. The whole thing was kind of a chaos and in this chaos order would be found.

Women were needed to carry Troyon offspring, yet they needed some variance of gene pool of male sperm to add variety to the mix on occasion. Males became some kind of expendable joke, a point of ridicule and torture. Females became an easily manufactured vessel for alien offspring whose birth meant death. The Troyons made camps that raised woman and a few boys that they lied to, spinning a yarn about how they were here to help. As time passed they would never figure out the lies, by sixteen they are ready to give them selves up and they were sent off for offspring duty. The Troyons had the attitude that this was fine, that this planet was seeded long ago and they were simply reaping its rewards.

Brea's eyes stung, exhaustion took grip. She felt as if she had been clubbed between the shoulder blades. Her eyes burned closed as she felt her way to the bed. Now as her body rested her mind was enlightened with a recent history of humankind, between the nightmares she had her respite of fond memories. Brea met Pete several times on the dream plane to plan a response after this first encounter.

The first Renaissance Dream shows a time of tragedy, and a scorching painful epoch for all women and for all of Earth—yes, but that scourge borne by women in the ability of procreating a gift used against its own humanity was deeply cruel, the cold empty chronology that smells of sulfur and cigarettes. The three witches Breanna, Naomi and Scarlet were all in Germany in 1592 starring into their black oil oracles foretelling the times that their future was already a part of.

The airfield was large, several large space vessels were boarding. The ships held thousands. Hearing snippets of conversations the fathers and grandmothers of betrothed women were being taken to meet up with their daughters and wives. The ships took off. The insides of the ships were electric with the emotion of reuniting families. Then with no warning large bay doors were opened, killing all the passengers, spilling them into the void of space. The ships would just go back and get another load of people and repeat the process.

A renegade band of military were said to have fled, taking a large toll on Troyons. It seemed that it was a large military exodus in space. Naomi sat there entranced, staring in her black oil pool on the table, and spoke, "Terror Wars were in full swing by 2015. Islamic fascism infiltrated every free country as walking dead. Suicide bombers wreaked havoc. Governments responded and bloodshed rocked civilization as the war of attrition raged as killing seeped through the populace. Censorship in this outbreak of attacks transformed all the media it into a government mouth piece.

A godsend, a race of extra-terrestrials reached out and informed us that we were already infiltrated. This statement should have raised red flags but we were grasping to solve our financial problems. American women worked hard to break glass ceilings. Isis on the other hand kept their women under wraps and underfoot. Then the Catholics started more and more as in the days of the witches hammer scorned women because of their fear of them that is why they give women no voice in their Church. Catholic priests stood on pulpits mocking women and their tears, scoffing at their dreams of becoming president. The government called them all haters and said their doctrines were flawed, the media whipping as hard as they could with a rainbow lash. Free speech and free thought were challenged. As in the past they classified woman as inherently evil and ill-willed. This made it easier for things to turn against them. Time passed and women were subjugated, which just lent credence to more subjugation. Visible skin became a crime; the unacceptable behavior of lifting oneself to a higher plateau was no longer tolerated. Objections were pacified by loads of fresh gold to finance a campaign of political power, the government now creating a nanny state. Enhancing a welfare state and controlling behavior more every day. Christianity and Islam vanished what seems like overnight, the males were slaughtered wholesale then females disappeared, their own faith used against them as a path to destruction. Christian woman were given to Troyons as a sign of sacrifice, Muslim woman were killed by males of their own family so as not to be stolen from them. The seculars gave service for a promise of cash for education or whatever was needed spun by the White House as the cool thing to do. Family waited for their purified female to return. They were constantly reassured all is well, this is necessary for the vanquishing of our enemies. There was some kind of coup, a lot more men died, and the insurgents were filtered out of the population. So, as free thinking women evanesced, so did the family. The death of the family then pulled the underpinnings of society, which sent the whole population into chaos.

More were swayed every day, yet there was this hardcore network of Department of Defense subcontractors that dug in to long obsolete and archaic work spaces, interiors and command bunkers that were 'need to know,' and the politicians didn't. These survivor civilians dug in deep and hid.

The size of the population shrank, first in half with excuses of sorting and information gathering to capture more terrorists. Unknown to each group the Troyon's made deals with all major groups and governments, promising everyone whatever they wanted. Politicians pleaded to the people for just a little more time, as loved ones never returned. Events changed from bad to worse as another renegade arm of military insiders went to interdict a Troyon sweep on the West Coast. This second coup was quickly squashed and revealed a thin yet impregnable exoskeleton that made Troyons almost invincible. The military ran to the stars to fight their enemy. Refitting old Troyon ships cast to the Earth at a dump site, Troyons looted other resources of the Earth to make new ships for themselves.

The remaining military, now hunted as traitors escaped to space, to do battle in the vacuum, the only thing that seemed to put the two on an even battleground. Even their exoskeletons are not safe in the vacuum of space. This mutiny also fed information to the Civil Defense League, and the remaining DOD contractors were just left to be hunted for sport, but strangely to the Troyons they just seemed to vanish. That Renegade band of military that fled took a large toll on Troyons in the vacuum of space. For those humans who didn't have the ability to leave the planet life was horrifying. The Trojans would rape them, they needed their uteruses for the live birth of their all male offspring that would eat through their hosts in a blood-curdling screaming birth. They used their technology to produce human female captives to birth more Troyon spawn.

There was one of three brothers, all of whom worked for the DOD, all eccentric and so close to that line of brilliance it was scary. The really scary part was Pete. He turned his own lab's works on himself trying to metamorphous himself to survive. Pete's over-indulgence led to a tempering of transformation for others so as not to overdo it as he did. Pete did this for his two daughters; his wife was one of the first never to return, taken in the middle of the night to bind his silence. Pete hid with his two daughters in the remains of Argonne labs.

Pete's sleepy eye opening slit the other eye buried in his pillow, starring at marvelous swifts' wings. He swiped off a piece of Chua cake on his finger. His daughter Amber had brought it earlier. Chua cake was the most nutritious confection created by a chef. Amber would always add more chemicals and supplements that would support the Morpheus nanotechnology metamorphosis. He had loaded his daughters with nanotech and given them chemical regiments to enhance their physical and mental capabilities. His experiments on himself guaranteed he did not push others too far. Pete knew releasing this technology into the remaining hiding population was his only choice, it was just scary how well it worked out. The tip of his index finger held a smattering of cake. He held his finger up as the fairy took a healthy bite. Her empyreal eyes starred at him lovingly, the soothing purrs of her wings mesmerized him. Her large teardropped eyes grew all pearl blue in low light to open the full corona to use any ambient light. In bright light it was a deep azure. Her dress was made of liquid platinum alloy. The strobes of platinum flashes were one of her cloaking mechanisms to guard her eloquent quickness. She was the smallest, yet fastest of the four fairy types. She would sit on your cupped hand like a half-moon.

This fairy's name was Rocket, named after the fairies that were designed in the comet series. She was the first. She kept her straight platinum hair carefully covering her burnt ear tips. Rocket's ears burn off because of her sheer speed. Pete held in his hand what looked like a florescent green tennis ball. Firmly lightly squeezing it, and then flipped it gently round, gripping it. The thick hairy tarantula climbed down to the table. It wasn't at all a natural tarantula; it was originally designed for secure communication, although it had a linear delivery system. The spiders made webs that were used for relay transmissions. The spiders evolved, first becoming aggressive to any threat to their human counterpart they also took on a few praying mantis characteristics for hunting and attacking. They helped interface the Nano mites and the humans. This tarantula was Pete's prototype and it had to be upgraded, almost a fatal mistake. So the responsibility of removing toxins from the body was also a duty of the spider. They were also constant companions, had learning ability and served their host.

The spiders were a caregiver to humans, since many more hours were spent alone due to the population blow-down. The spider tied all survival protocol, the life suits, sojourns, and need to know information. The tarantula started tapping on the table with its legs. Feeling left out, the fairy hovered down and stood next to it stroking its leg. "My little friends," Pete thought.

The fairy quickly hovered, the spider quickly scurried to its resting place in the back of Pete's head just above the hairline. Someone was close to the door. Pete stood flicking the ball in his hand as he started to wind up a pitch. The ball contained genetic material supplied by Pete. All males donated, and the fairies would collect it and deliver it to the proper survivor cell in the network. Rocket started doing loops building speed. Just as the door opened, the tennis ball came screaming through the opening crack, as the fairy followed at breakneck speed.

"Dad!" Amber exclaimed. "You know you're not supposed to take the birds out of the aviary." The comet class fairy also has in its stealth arsenal a receptor interceptor. The pulse enters the eye and changes the fairy's appearance at the ocular receptor level before the brain reconfigures it. The RI pulse disguises the fairy. Hence they are not what they seem. Just lately dad seemed so distant and his delusions which were concerning his daughters after they almost lost him a year ago because he didn't upgrade his spider. The girls thought he was just over-medicating. Most people looked up into the heavens at night and dreamed of flying through the stars, or feel warm romance, seemed Pete would see the blackness between the stars, and know that to be the dark matter. Those distant bright spots where universes met generated dark energy. Then he succeeded and figures a way to harness that dark matter energy that lay between the stars. He also theorized that dark matter was in the smallest of cosmic spaces, that being the space between atoms. That star stuff we're all made of also has an order of function in the ethereal plane, and somehow it is channeled to the mito-chondria. At this level the mitochondria directed the interface between the two realms, enabling this realm to live, and direct dark energy feeding man at the cellular level if no food would be available. The powering of the life suit and all other new things! So, Pete's techno survival cells, (cells in this case a group of individuals in a larger network of survivors and these were known as the uncles) would lose memory of how the advances were made once these advances became self-replicating, but they worked and had a physics of their own. Pete exposed himself to every body enhancing drug and Nano mite experiment he could devise that boosted his brainpower and physical prowess. This started a progression to his near death, solved by a simple upgrade of software. Whatever worked on him he shared with the precious survivors.

Breanna's sights were now set on her return to an Earth par-allel. Brea entered her Sojourn when she was hiding in the tree roots, the spiders folded time and space around the sojourn and she ended up in a green space by the expressway back in her own time using the parallel corridor. Flanked by her oak walking stick and her white birch wand, crowned with her witch's halo, she searched the dressing table mirror oracle for a road called 'Veterans' Parkway'.

The twisted ribbons of the old highway had succumbed to the aging of an evolving planet. The image took her to an overpass that she concentrated on. This was her only chance to perceive her destination. Brea wore her halo with a dark hood over it, and bejeweled the top of her walking stick with a fist-sized Blue Amethyst Geode.

The spider split and opened the door. As she ventured outside the Sojourn the cold rain struck horizontally. The spider united and was hit with an information load from the environment bringing it up to date with the current situation. As it snuggled itself in back of her ear against her scalp it assured her that it would alarm her and hide her in case of Troyons. The Troyons were interested in the lore of the land and would have this phenomenon of us blinking in and out as a ghost. Brea heard faintly playing in the back of her head the words from a song in the Wizard of Oz "We're Off to See the Wizard." Somehow she thought this meant something.

The rain warmed. It seemed to have a cleansing effect on Brea. Then rain stopped, ushering in a steady wind. The guard rail was rusted and crusted with oxides. The asphalt reminisce separated the plant growth. Walking to the top of the clover leaf, she saw her direction west. She started to walk. Houses and buildings were quietly decaying. The caw of crows and the chatter of Monk Parrots were heard sporadically. She knew they were on her side, like having a flock of familiars. Her spider started sending her messages with the location she was searching for, she was on the right track. She walked steady for a day, encountering fair weather and those birds. Brea walked near a small stream. The shadow on the ground shocked her at first. The bird shadow on the ground looked prehistoric, pterodactyl like, yet as her head jolted up it was a Blue Heron. Brea's walk brought her to a culvert, where a heron sat on a chunk of fence fishing the man-made stream below it. Brea slowed her pace. The bird merely held his beak to his chest and never took his eyes off her, the long eyes just peering at her. As she passed him he gave a bit of a beak wiggle and a nasal release of air, almost as if in disbelief at seeing her.

Brea then found her way to a dozen large refinery holding tanks and a maze of pipes and docks. Her spider began to dance quickly on her ear lobe. "Go ahead then and open it," she thought. The spider jumped out and split. Grasping onto the zipper of time the curtain opened and she entered, and none too soon the Troyons had arrived. She sat at her dressing table watching them in the reflection of the mirror, walking around with scanners and other gadgets for searching. The Troyons began to pound on the long maze of pipes, the sound seeming to go on forever. Breanna stayed in her Sojourn for two days until the threat was gone.

The green sign read "Veterans' Parkway." The pitted guard rail was on the short winding ribbon of reclaimed road. Bittersweet nightshade, a climbing plant with loose flattering clusters also called deadly nightshade, is used in London to combat witch-craft; it was growing in the Yoke of a Honey Locust tree just off Veterans' Parkway. As Brea looked she saw the storage tank of the Lake Michigan water distribution. Her brain skipped, which stopped her in her tracks. It felt like a déjà vu moment that gave her memory a spark of insight she had no memory of! A large domed brick and concrete water holding tank had no sign of entry. An elongated brick building was close by the tank, which were the water pumping station, on the not so distant ridge stood a beautiful tall brick home with an observation enclosure topping it. Breanna walked around the tank, trying to figure out why she needed to be there.

The tank had beautiful brick work. Brea's spider came into her hand. It shot out several feet of web, dancing in the light breeze as she walked around the tank, then the web hit something it pinged like a tuning fork. The spider jumped and split itself in two but instead of opening Brea's sojourn it unlocked the enterance to the tank. Brea then stepped inside the spider corridor, closing the passage, and the room became lit. There were two hundred jars of different sizes, each with a developing fairy. Each jar was connected to a black box with a silver umbilical cord, on each box was a spider. Breanna knew what she had to do now: entice two hundred Earth spirits to use these vehicles to assist mankind and themselves to exist.

The posse had Scarlet tied to a tree, her arms tied around the tree, a rope around each wrist as they used a branch to tighten and twisting it in the rope pulling her shoulders from her sockets. The excruciating pain her body was enduring set off the brain's defense mechanisms, trying to separate her body and soul. The captain stroked her head as he ordered the harlot bitch defiled.

"This witch must be tortured before we burn her so that we may save her soul," the captain said. He and three others stayed behind as he sent three others to gather wood for their witch roast.

The four men that stayed behind stripped her they began to tie her back at the ankles, harshly groping her. The pain of her wrenched body put her in and out of consciousness; it was like watching herself as being next to herself. The men in their repugnant zeal began tugging at her, trying to elicit a response. Then she felt nothing her eyes would not even open. The razor sharp serpent tail skewered the three men, the first man looking down at the spade shaped tip through his sternum as it cut sideways opening their hearts and chests. The captain died in disbelief as the sea eagle billed demon simply snacked on his head the body falling motionless to the ground.

The Russian Sea Eagle billed, dragon headed, spade tailed demon morphed back into a large dark skinned man. He so gently unbound her from the tree, his confidence in every cut of her bonds; she gained strength by his guarded touch. He held her close as he straightened her shoulders she dropped limp into his arms. Hector sniffed deep: she smelt so sweet, even though she had been through such great strife. Her scent came through his nostrils, and he tasted Scarlet's magic on his tongue. Hector cradled her in his arms, changed forms and took to the air. He spied a deserted cottage, its roof in disrepair. He took her inside and placed her in a corner. Rummaging around Hector found a container. He flew a short distance and collected some water. Upon his return he cleaned her and covered her in a makeshift bed. The former residents had left in a hurry.

Naomi was young, only eleven years old. She remembers that day when her father entrusted her to her uncle so they could escape, but their escape was into the clutches of the past. The men that killed her uncle, the man that she was entrusted to was murdered. These witch hunters believed the uncle was a warlock raising a rising triad of blood witches. Naomi was the younger cousin of Brea and Scarlet. Their father's death so full of trauma, there sisters believed Naomi to be dead and Naomi believed Brea and Scarlet dead as well.

Naomi hunted with the wolf and combed cinder through her hair to tame its fire red. She used pitch and mud to hide her ivory complexion. Naomi hid her emerald eyes by looking down. She used hides of animals for her sparse commerce. Naomi also was haunted. At times she thought her cousins were with her with a ghostly shiver, needless to say a foretelling they were still alive. Naomi's witchy ways were with her, yet hidden just below what she could not reach. Alone Naomi did not know of her full magic potential, a glimmering sixth sense of gut feeling and awareness until her sixteenth birthday a woman came to her in a dream and told her a bodyguard would have to stay with her now. That morning she awoke with a Griffin tattoo encompassing a portion of her torso and looked as if he were sleeping next to her as she slept at night. As she lay naked tossed in a cage waiting to be burned at the stake the guards brought hot irons trying to burn off the dragon. The guards would simply drop the irons, because they grew so cold to the touch it would burn. Some guards said they even saw the tattoo move.

A simple look up toward a haunting voice she had heard as she passed a man in the market. Naomi's pure green eyes gave her away when she glanced at the man, looking up because she heard the voice of that man that killed her uncle. Captured and stripped to reveal her Snallygaster fusion tattoo, Naomi's fate was sealed with this demonic art. "Burn it, burn it all." Naomi heard the voices as they passed to spit on her. Naomi prayed that night to her Father in Heaven. "Dear Father in Heaven, he who seeds the womanhood of the World, I pray that your divine wisdom instills in me the fortitude, I your daughter will soon need to endure. Dear Father you are my shepherd. I shall not want, in verdant pastures you give me repose, by restful waters you lead me and this refreshes my soul. You shall lead me to the path of righteousness. Even though I shall walk in the valley of shadow of death, I shall feel no evil, for you are with me with your rod and your staff that gives me courage. You prepare a table before me in the sight of my foes, you anoint my head with oil; my cup overflows. Only goodness and love shall follow me all the days of my life, and I shall dwell in my Father's house forever." Naomi's tattoo was a friend for her on those cold nights, at those times of self-doubt. Her demon was no monster to her but a creation of her Father's protection; surely it is the ignorance and malice of these people that are the monster? Every time fear began to creep in her thoughts she would pray and fill her thoughts like Joan of Arc did with her Father in heaven.

The two burly men pulled her from her cage. They slapped at her head, not wanting the witch to look at them and hex them. They bound her with brass around her wrists and ankles, a long rope tied around her arms so they could drag her through the street to her execution. Dragging her through the dirt people lined her path to defile her by throwing rotting food and feces at her. Naomi wondered who was screaming and crying in pain, Naomi then realized it was not another witch to be burned that she was hearing, but she was hearing herself. Naomi looked down on the scene, the mob jeered and taunted the pain had pushed her spirit from her body. Naomi's faith in the spirit allowed her to stand next to the pain.

Naomi was pulled from the dusty road and tied to the stake, bundles of wood tossed at her feet, followed by torches. Then through the skies she saw a dragon spirit come alongside of her spirit above the fire. Blades of dragon wings shone their energy outline in the fire.

"It is not your time Naomi, take my hand and I will lead you to your sister." Hector's spirit reached out. Naomi saw him as her guardian angel. They headed toward her mortal self, body slumped fire building in bundles of wood at her stake. Naomi woke in her sister Scarlet's arms as she tended her wounds. Her memory was a vague scary dream, the dreams a haunting reminder of the endurance of the human soul.

Making a fire in the fireplace he made short work of a few rabbits and put them in a pot above the fire. Hector stared at Scarlet for a while. She rested comfortably for he had blocked her pain receptors. Her ordeal left no permanent damage as he used the power of his demon eyes to see through her. He fashioned a garment for her. The rabbits stewed he would use the broth to feed her to help her regain her strength. Hector spoke to her as if she was awake to try and stimulate her and get her conscious. He held her up and placed a spoon to her lips, getting her to sip the broth. "Scarlet," he spoke quietly to her. "Scarlet your magic reminds me of my parents' scarlet hearted passion, what a beautiful name Scarlet!"

Her eyes opened and her voice was barely audible. "Who are you?" Scarlet's query was short but open.

Hector could not resist. He couldn't remember the last time he had a captive audience.

"I am Hector. I am one of two demons who are your bodyguards at your sister's behest, but before we reunited you with your sisters we must find the plasma tool that was sent here before we go back." Scarlet was confused. All she heard was "reunite with her sisters," which put her at ease, but she questioned his use of the plural 'sisters.' She sipped a bit more broth and slipped off to sleep.

Hector looked at the night sky, the spirits of the Earth spoke to him enlightening him on the distance and direction of his journey.

"If the Earth were different she and I would be hardened adversaries," Hector thought, looking at her sleeping—restful—content. This one has deep white sorcery powers. Hector remembers his last encounter with one of these souls. It shot its own soul with an astral arrow and revealed a beast that almost overpowered him. This darker hidden force in man scared Hector, the father had given man a very powerful soul. A white sorcerer's soul is strong. The darkness that lives deep in an enlightened soul is the most powerful because it has to overcome the goodness within it and lashes out wildly.

Scarlet rustled as Hector stared out the window. "Eggs would be a good breakfast; I'll raid a few birds in the morning." Hector heard the beating of a large bat's wing, but it was a shape shifting dark essence, an earthen essence. It called to him in a polite voice asking an audience.

"You pierce my night and don't announce yourself. Surely if there is any aid you need on this plane I will be more than glad to help." The large bat spoke as it landed close and awkwardly walked toward Hector.

"Your alliance is at a cost!" Hector retorted. "I owe you nothing."

"I have information for you. I know your mission, this task will be assured its fulfillment. Possibly you may complete your quest alone, but I know you alone cannot save the witch's lost sister Naomi and retrieve the plasma all in time to get to your portal for an extraction back to your proper time." She yawned and stumbled around a bit. "That witch you hide."

"Yes! What about her?" Hector said forcefully.

"Her sister Breanna back in your proper time who wear's the six pointed star ring plans to help two hundred earthen essences escape," she stated.

"This matters to you how?" Hector queried.

"I am not one of the two hundred." Her head shook. "I need passage for me and four of my allies." Hector knew he had to help her for these spirits forged that dark lauded place in man, and a balance with his forces should be maintained.

"I will gain you passage for your assistance here Lil," Hector said.

"Thank you Hector, my legion here are now at you beck and call," Lilith said, her head shaking, showing her teeth. "May I shift to myself?" she asked feeling uncomfortable in the bat's skin standing next to Hector.

"Sure you may, and thank you for asking. Remember though I too shift and I may look human, but do not forget I am a strong and powerful Griffin so please," he smiled devilishly, "don't insult me and try to seduce me." The tall alabaster skinned woman stood in front of him. Lilith's hair was long, straight and raven black. Her eyes burned red. Lilith's sheer white garments make her look ghostlike. She smiled shyly revealing her slightly enlarged canine teeth.

"Wouldn't think of it my sisters are in trouble in this time and in hers." She gestured toward Scarlet. "I see a Matriarchal society ahead if I can help my sisters reconstitute themselves. Adam put forth his case and did not want to shepherd man's view in an equal partnership and for that I have paid a great price, but my sisters shall not be put down by these alien men's deviance." Lilith's eyes were flaring red.

"Calm yourself! If not for this invasion we would be joined in immortal combat. Strange as it may seem, we need mankind to separate us and the creator so that we may be defined." Hector spoke trying to understand the reason for this plight, wondering why his creator left this mission in his hands, that he and his brother help mankind.

"Just because we exist on the dark side of nature does not mean we are evil," Lilith spoke. "For without the dark there would be no light.

Then she descended her name Morgan. She was six feet tall and white, but not alabaster white, more of a powder white. The only other color was a void of color. A black was the only highlight, black that matches her eyes—cold crude oil pools. Her wings were large. The elbow of the wing arched above her head as she stood. A lengthy fringe was close to the ground. The texture of her feathery wings was soft if stroked down with the grain like cedar tree, sharp and prickly opposite the grain. She was holding a white birch wand with a glossy black grounding stone on the top, her dress a flowing wrapped gown which had a coffin satin appearance to it.

"Lilith the Sphinx has found the meteor," Morgan spoke, her gaze fixed on Hector.

"Bring the meteor for Hector, Morgan; he must first save the sister witch Naomi before she burns." Morgan nodded and streaked straight up. "I marked this Naomi witch on her sixteenth birthday. Use the arrow spell of this Scarlet witch to save her," Lilith spoke and morphed back into a bat and flew away.

Hector burst into the hovel and immediately began to speak.

"Scarlet your sister Naomi lives. I need your astral arrow incantation to channel to her and save her." Scarlet rose as quickly as she could. Pulling a razor from her mouth she sliced her hand. She wiped the blood on Hector's lips. She guided him by his shoulders and faced him toward the fire. Scarlet spied a worn broom and grabbed it by its pecan handle. She put it in Hector's hand.

"Point this toward the fire and summon hell fire to blaze your path," Scarlet explained quickly. From the core of the handle an angry hell fire shot in the fire place and shot up from the chimney to the sky. Scarlet then voiced an incantation.

"My soul shall be the bow; my actions the arrow to pierce your spirit and release from it the beast you need to be to complete your task and save my sister. Mother may your daughter's precious blood lead this demon to my sister and bring her to me, for this demon Hector has been tasked to protect me and my sisters, I humbly ask your assistance so mote it be." Scarlet then pushed Hector toward the hell fire and the fire swallowed him whole. Before Hector could think another thought he was hovering above the execution of Naomi. Hector knew he was in astral form as he watched Naomi's soul rise above her still connected by the silver cord. Hector willed himself to her and flew down inside her. He gave that silver cord a good solid tug and her soul cascaded back down to her body. As soon as she entered herself he grabbed her and pushed out through her tattoo as the town leaders cheered the growing flames.

The Griffin emerged, merging Naomi into him. Those people that were ordered to watch the execution and had no taste for this witch burning ran away in fear, while the conspirators and zealots were frozen in their panic-stricken places. Hector was in his full power, even more so with the unleashing of the astral arrow. He was the most powerful demon. His wings kept pounding the air, a bellows fanning the flames of the pyre until he moved so much air to gain altitude. Hector roasted to death all who were frozen in guilt.

The fire waned as he flew high above the smoke, rising toward them. Hector hovered, looking at the stars and trying to get a bearing back to the shack. Hector stayed aloft as he saw someone approach. As she got closer he saw that it was Morgan. She flew up to him and spoke. "Hello Hector, you seemed so busy I retrieved the plasma meteor." Morgan used it like a nail file against one of Hector's prawns of his claw until the plasma migrated to it. "Follow me; I will take you back to your witch." She flew due east and Hector was close behind. Hector felt Naomi's soft flesh inside his astral self. It was such a contrast from his leathery scaled body and though she had been through much, the brightness of her soul thanked him so for saving her in a thankful gush of universal love. Hector felt his heart and quickly countered the emotion. He conveyed to her, "Father has given a task and I intend to fulfill that, do not let down your guard, we still have much to do!" Morgan shot a fire light toward the dugout. Hector saw a magical red smoke billowing from the chimney, Scarlet stood outside with arms uplifted, and Hector headed right for the chimney stack. What was left of the hovel blew out soot and stone blasted the remaining structure. A red glow died back, the hell fire now cold.

"Naomi! Hector!" Scarlet called continuously as she entered the impact site. Walking out from the rubble was Hector in his full armor, about nine feet tall, spikes on elbows, knees, and shoulders, horns covering the head and facing forward, a trident tail and ribbed wings of razor scales. Hector cradled Naomi in his arms. She molded between his sharp armor plates feeling secure in his stone embrace.

"Up on my back and tend to your sister," Hector commanded. "We don't have much time and must take to the sky." Hector went into full Snally Gaistor mode helped the sisters to his neck and began to fly to find the angels' stairway.

As Hector flew Scarlet was so blissful to see her sister. She began to speak to her, "Oh Naomi I thought you were dead." Naomi was covered in soot and her hair was a burnt mat. "Let me see your face." As Scarlet looked at her she opened her eyes. "Sister, your eyes!" Naomi's eyes had become green lizard eyes like Hectors'.

Three

⇒ THERAPY ⇐

"During times of universal deceit, telling the truth becomes a revolutionary act." George Orwell

A cool breeze skipped over the lake caressing exposed skin, bathed warm in sunlight: slight goose bumps. It was a picturesque day, children in the distance playing on bicycles, the sound of rubber braking on gravel, with the faint chattering of playful voices. Small boats methodically trawled the lake. The view from the deck looking out into the....

"Pete! Morning sir." His accent was very Americanized British. "Kyle ... Kyle Waters," Kyle said, reaching out his hand. He smiled as they shook hands; this is my new assistant, Pete thought. Pete's therapy was to get everything down as he remembered it.

"Sit; Sit down," Pete said, leading him to the table on the back deck. Kyle placed his laptop down, plugging in his solar panel charger, pulling a small digital recorder from his pocket and placing it on the table. Kyle placed a folded over pad of legal paper in from of him and placed a pen on top. Pete un-holstered his weapon, Pete wielded a Colt 357 Magnum with a six-inch barrel and placed that on the table. A simple weapon, so it seemed, blue steel with walnut handles. Kyle took notice.

"Nice revolver," Kyle said, studying Pete.

Pete just started right in talking. "Plasma has the inherent capability of emotional demeanor of its user emotions of fear, revenge, anger; all act as a catalyst to excite the plasma. The excited plasma is ignited by dark matter energy. A charge is then discharged in the manner to eliminate the threat to the user. Tempered or terminal and raw anger can make it a terrible event for the enemy." Pete got that far-away look in his eye.

"Sword discharged plasma has been known to sanitize an acre round buffer. Once weapons are plasma enhanced they become a Troyon killer. The Samurai sword was the blade of choice. The sword could then discharge and direct a plasma stream, destroying the threat." Pete raised the gun to Kyle's head and pulled the trigger; nothing happened, except Kyle's Adam's apple jumped up and down at the sound of the hammer hitting dry. "No threat no discharge. The great equalizer, the pistol, or a sword, club, or your bare hands, they all can kill our enemies. I remember when murders from shootings were spiking in the cities; the political controllers blamed the gun. A wise man once told me if you kill a man you take away everything that man has achieved and everything he will achieve. Everything he has or will have, just think of that for a moment. Then to rob a man and shoot him dead for a crumbled five dollars in his pocket after leaving the gin mill, this is not a gun problem, this is a problem of society—respect of life and worth of life. A clause in the American Constitution eroded by its own government's political greed steals the fruits this constitution bestows upon all men, to enrich the political class. The power drunken bastards, this vain oligarchy treat a pliable media to make a world mask to hide their treachery. They send in great soldiers to die, not for protection of one's nation but for a political goal. They fail in their morals for the respect of life, as for the worth of life... well, dead in that instance is worth more than alive. Beliefs that babies are not human until they leave the hospital, some believe not until five when they are socialized. Whatever their belief that should not be able to steal life, then take the discarded fetuses and part them out to the highest bidder, and the government partially finances these abortions with the citizens' own tax money. What species kills its own offspring like this, in a lab coat of medical deception, a lifesaving guise for the baby, this is considered civilized. Society is abandoning its morality to television and the media mask, so before blaming the way a man dies, weigh the situation's moral underpinnings. So you see the Troyons had no problem inserting themselves in mankind's demise; once a thing is broken and never fixed it decays away." Pete's eyes grew distant, sunken and sad; a blanket of sorrow enveloped him. Then like the snap of a finger, his demeanor changed and he again began to speak as he rubbed his chiseled brow.

"They are all smart weapons: weapon does not fire if I am not in jeopardy; when I am in peril it kills. Looks like a Colt, far from it though. The entire six shot cylinder emits a highly excited plasma projectile, with pin point accuracy or air burst area sanitation, split polished trigger for hair quality, walnut handle, plasma reinforced for almost inexhaustible battle situation. It reloads off its target. It's a Troyon killer; it consumes its kill's residue, plain and simple." Peter placed the pistol down on the table, handle toward Kyle. "My first enhancement boosted my intelligence; we all did it, all who were left—felt deserted with nothing left to lose. We knew every-one could not be saved by the government; in fact the governments were the problem, so we had to save ourselves. I remember that argument well between my daughters and me." Pete thoughts drifted back to that day.

"Who do you think you are some kind of god?" Amber questioned standing there with her sister Kayla not liking what their dad was talking about or the path he was taking.

"I'm not on a dark path, but when astrophysics and the bible are so closely correlated I believe in miracles." Pete began gesturing and motioning as if on a stage, imploring them to see his way. His daughters began wondering if their dad had already started his drug regimen. "Let your minds try and wrap around this one girls. The known universe, all matter that exists in it, came to being in one tenth of a second, everything in that big bang. Both of you close your eyes a minute." Pete's eyes closed as he motioned to the girls to do the same. "Those voids, before the starting of time, that pre-bang empty etiolates canvas, just think of that now and open your eyes." When Pete saw his girls' eyes open he went into a dithyramb. "Then there was light, Genesis. All that we see and is came into existence. Galaxy upon galaxy and the darkness between them, the entire known universe present, in the time it took for you to open your eyes." Pete's azure eyes looked into his daughters' like eyes and he simply stated, "And all I want to do is pull a rabbit out of a hat." His daughters saw the desperation of the day and agreed to help their father be a magician. Pete just continued on talking, it was his therapy after all. "The physical aspect we created Nano robots with analyzing and evolution capacity and interfaced it with our spiders, the spider transmitter which embeds itself in a person's scalp and makes a connection to the hypothalamus the spiders hairy covering is actually an antenna array allowing them to communicate between each other in a very low and narrow band, giving less range but keeping them connected. As web transfer sites were set everyone was soon connected. The spiders also acted as filters, trapping and not transmitting thoughts to be scrutinized by each other (example Jack has a private sexual fantasy that detail fantasy would not be transmitted)." Pete's eyes widened as he leaned forward; just as quickly he sat back, looking sad, blank. "The alloy for that weapon is the same I use on our aircraft. I invented it, yet I can't remember how I found the formula for it." Pete waved his finger in circles above the walnut handle grips. "Those grips were given to me by a fairy named Tori just before the Troyon final battle, right around my birthday." Pete's eyes welled with tears. "Tori I ... I believe she carved the handles from the wood of her home, she resided in a walnut tree. I think that what she was trying to convey, a token of her home and mine. Tori is an empath and she has no vocal capabilities." Pete's eyes glassed over.

"A penny for your thoughts?" Kyle said engaging Pete, trying to keep him lucid.

"Can't talk about them anymore, they have their secrets, we all have secrets." Pete whispered softly to himself then he sat straight and began talking in an even tone. "It was after the second time I juiced (slang for drug enhancement therapy, high protein and metal for the nanos and synaptic acceleration for brain development). Pete was trying to convince his daughters about the procedure, and well he got laid up with a hundred and four fever, he was watching an old movie, *The Bride of Franken-stein*. That is when Pete had an epiphany; in the movie they grew entities in jars, but he would not want them soulless, so he would do the same, grow them in jars, developing a secret legion of fairies, but he needed a witch to give them earthen spirits." Pete eyes intensely gazed at the monitor. *The Bride of Frankenstein* was playing. The scientist pulled the jars from the case. Pete's eyes closed. "That's it," he said to himself sitting in his dream world.

The room was full of jars ranging from one pint wide mouth mason jars to five gallon water cooler bottles. Pete's mind raced in a hurried pace of fact and formulas, launching another synapse jump, chemicals humming in his veins. The only consolation is there are no pain nerves in the brain as nanos rewired areas. It was all there staring at him through his mind's eye, his brain linked to the cosmic conscience. The answers to all problems were just there and he felt himself the catalyst to start these events and see them to fruition. First Pete pushed human limits by introducing Nano mites directly into humans' bone marrow to change the stem cells and allow them to reproduce, allowing injuries to heal or change the DNA to enhance the human. The largest change was in the babies, known as dirt babies, their stealth capabilities their only defense. Babies would grow better organs, drugs were produced to achieve peak performance to push the limits of muscle and fight. A synergy of man's technology and man was at its infancy. Then true AI spiders. The uncles were contractors for the DOD.

Michael was the head of NACHOS—Nano composite optical ceramic Nano scale Architectures for Coherent hyper-optic sources. Pete was the project coordinator for the NAV Nano Air Vehicle, Molecular Level Robots Program on Medicine Tech and Society. Defense Advanced Research Projects Agency Human Assisted Neural Devices Program Genetic Robotic Nano Technology.

The two brothers, also metallurgists, designed signature metals. These metals' properties bent radio waves around vessels and also light, which gave it true daytime invisibility. These technologies, once a distant fiction, were magical. Then mixing the magic physics of another realm of your destination was a force to be reckoned with.

Troyon reached out to pie in the sky politicians who were promised quick results and led by fresh gold for their coffers. This 'Godsend Race' of extra-terrestrials' plan was to get access to our populations so they could sort out those sleepers and put the enemy back on their heels. The liberal attitude of immigration in Europe and America led to a steady infiltration of Islamic extremism, which corroded the existing norms and led to a fear of one's neighbors. ISIS marched and spread its influence, more were swayed every day, yet there were these hardcore networks of Department of Defense subcontractors that dug in to long obsolete and archaic work spaces, interiors and command bunkers.

"Good skeptical generals were purged with framed marital affairs and computer profile blunders that left in place a flock of sheep. They could not coup so they hit and ran. The soldiers were targeted because of their tactical knowledge and space was their only escape, knowing their running would allow survivors to hide. They did not know the full plan other than to find the Troyon home world, use the vacuum of space to their advantage and know they will someday return to see mankind's liberation."

Catholic priests at first were reprimanded for tearing into woman, enlarging a fear of what these men thought of woman. Islam lent credence to the subjugation of woman, then ISIS doctrines leading to the bullying of woman. Times were going to get real bad for girls real soon. The problem with the Muslins was that they wanted to subjugate their own woman and for that, that population paid a dear price for they were decimated, for the Troyons goals were also women, so for the most part that population was scrubbed clean. Western culture rang it as a new offense in the war on terror. The West had enough problems, if you were against woman surrogating their pregnancies to the Troyons you were a sexist. It was a woman's body she could do whatever she wanted. The payout was big money and the president himself said, "Woman can do what they want with their bodies, and I have written an executive order that no federal or state taxes will be taken from this income. This procedure is safe I guarantee it." No one ever showed up for their free college education. Politicians pleaded for just a little more time, as loved ones disappeared. Events changed from bad to worse as a renegade arm of retired generals moved to interdict a Troyon sweep on the West Coast. The rebellion was quickly squashed and revealed a thin yet impregnable exoskeleton that made the Troyans invincible for now.

The remaining generals' fifth column, now hunted as terrorists (Troyons blamed the military for assassination of the president), escaped to space to do battle in the vacuum, the only thing that appeared to put the two on an even battlefield. The military scrounged its new fleet from the Troyon discarded ships, as the Troyons rebuilt a new fleet from their Earth plunder. An idea of mistrust leaned toward the military a cut and run mental misconception, the remainder of people were told they were deserted by the military. The Civil Defense League, the remaining

DOD contractors, who didn't have the ability to leave the planet, hunkered down. This information was at least horrifying. The Troyons were slaughtering the male population wholesale, only allowing enough to remain alive for a diverse genetic pool. The female population was its need and target. The Troyon's would woo them at first and as time passed they just raped them. They needed their uteruses for the live birth of their all male offspring that would devour part of its host in a blood curdling screaming birth. The Troyons long ago had destroyed its female genes. This species was all male and utilized others for their propagation.

Pete was that missing link. That link where he could no longer let the situation around him mold the future for the future was that bleak. Pete seeks the dark energy algorithm, therefore he super-boosted his brain and turned his unused cell space into mass storage. A prisoner class of female humans bred in artificial uteruses that, shortly after their sixteenth birthday, are used for the gestation of a Troyon son and its mother to be ripped apart and be snacked on after its birth. And just think, when the Troyons came they spoke of saving all life. A human male population depleted to a sperm pool only large enough to avoid inbreeding.

The Memorial Day started hot; then grew hot and humid. The night before storm after storm came through. Pete struggled that morning to open the pool with his eight year old that was pulling the pool ballast through the flooded yard as if that were a game. The Sun hurt Pete's eyes, or was it the light? He remember watching years ago the 'Prisoner' with that damn bubble always chasing them back. The scene kind of reminded him of that. That's all it was, though, a memory. Pete lifted himself from the floor, he was laying in about two inches of water. "I know I see my daughter when she is eight but I do not remember her name. I look down on my own forearm I see the optic implants disguised by tattoos." Pete said as he scanned his secret world around him.

"My brain is hard wired-hot; not to mention my hot body. Memories recall to me in a dull painful stabbing. I need to endure this for my own sanity's sake and the events as I remember them for history sake. There has been so much rewriting of end times, all it takes is a generation and the cooperation of the educational system. Media repeated disinformation engrains itself so deeply it gives the past the same hazy look as the future. The media beguiles you as the kakistocracy regulates you, having the effect of unintended consequences tearing societies and cultures, creating a culture of government, its corruption ripe for the picking." Pete's eyes began fluttering, a series of light coughs seemed to stop the eye tremors, yet Peter became blank.

"Hey there buddy," Kyle said in his best American voice. He went to shake Pete's elbow but was stopped by his voice.

"Motion-energy that was my problem, then I can have a place to hide," Peter blurted out as Kyle slipped back into his seat. "The basis of the dark energy and its delivery system is the connection through the dark energy void, those spaces between electrons that are the super intermolecular highway of energy delivery. With ninety percent of the dark matter in the universe unexplained, the influence of the war and the techno-altruistic evolution of man, the jolt of speeding technology and the immense task of sorting it relevancy, to tinker with drugs, human from that point on were implanted with chips to enhance us to endure the overlords. Man's boosted brain imagines were created."

"Once I found the right combination to the second pair of the foundation of the cosmos's new world appeared to me, that world that bases our legends and fantasies on. A world that shared our world, we only needed the lens to interact and know that our futures are interwoven. Finding this realm opened our eyes to the dark matter and its energy and how it can be used. It also showed us a compatible planet that the seed of humanity failed in, now it was ready to receive us with open arms. The original spiders were ninety percent claytronic quartz. This technology with the fairies made a stealth type of world still looking like a destroyed civilization but where man needed was totally operational and in fine repair. The fairies called this deception Fata Morgana. That interface with the hyper thalamus and spider was a communication connection. The artificial intelligence that mutated was based on the compassion nerve that hard wires compassion in the brain for species' survival. Once merged and connected to the dark energy conduit, well it really let the genie out of the bottle. Mankind would ask, 'Is it necessary for our survival?' If it works I will be hailed as a man of foresight, if it fails we shall all be dead or subjugated with a factious history, so my only choice is to act!"

The dark matter energy is channeled in the core magna of the Earth, the Earths' magma is the containment chamber for the dark energy fission reaction that interfaces with the spiders through the lightning plumes that come up from the Earth's dark energy networks through the high atmosphere lighting phenomenon. Through the dark energy interwoven at the cellular level this network of delivery dark matter energy within the molecular structure therefore is insulated and the energy is safely and securely transferred to this physical world as a conduit of energy. This conduit alternate realm highway core running through was a new energy source. This also fuels the alternate human condition that was forced upon humankind. The Chicago was used by Pale Skin to initiate the dark matter energy using the energy from its reactors as a pony motor. This reaction fueled the engrained Earthen plan of those who threw caution to the wind and saw that the chance of survival free of this tyranny is more important than the monkey on your back of unintended consequences of drugs and enhancements that you endure, whichever you think is less formidable. A direct power source to survive if separated from food, but you were always encouraged to eat. Your metabolism was raced through puberty and then you were in a limbo of life between eighteen and twenty-five.

Once the veil of man's reality had been torn asunder, survival of humanity was paramount, yet we didn't see, or didn't want to recognize that which stared us in the face. Humans were then hidden in the realms of miracles and myths. The dark energy realm is shutting off the forward advance of time, and folding back onto itself, these pockets are formed once inside, and the slit is closed and the fabric of the spider's web acts as a border filament between reality and the vestibule of the wormhole. Nanos mites also like the webbing as their new fabric. Basically it's a cut in the corridor of this universe that the dark energy opens and housekeeping is set up in this corridor of time, a no-place place. This is the realm that apparitions disappear to, the secrets of fairies of how they hid and hide. This was our sojourn.

A witch by the name of Brea communicated with Pete. Pete facilitated secrets for their survival, in a series of dreams and waking visions, where he struck his deal for his legion of two hundred fairies of earthen spirits. How good it felt to be able to sleep and be unafraid, tucked in a sojourn. The other enhancement from the spider was the life suit. The webbing produced by the spiders formed a very durable bullet proof material. This material was used to produce the life vest tailored to each individual with applications that conformed to the need of the user by the interface of the spider and the Nano mite. The material also took in and transferred these energies in and converted (recycled) the energy to a usable form. "How?" Pete answered his own query. "Necessity; and a bunch of NASA and other engineers who knew they had a chance juicing and taking that leap, were tired of acting as tour guides, doing garage sales on gantries, talking about the good old days when advances were timely and many. They knew their best days were not behind them in a dying subservient species, but with their talents bestowed upon them by their father in heaven to fight for their survival; their existence was a future as bright as they could dream. How most people would look up into the night sky would have thoughts of flying to the stars; these men would look up and see the blackness between the stars and ask, "What a powerful force these black voids have keeping these stars apart, how can I harness this?" Pete continued speaking.

"During my metamorphosis and bouts of high fever I believe my essence, my soul astral projected. I found these times rather restful. Since I had no brain in tow I was an emotional being. The calculus was replaced with chaos, no longer looking at the mathematical proof but, emotionally awestruck by the expanding universe. There I met a witch named Breanna. She was one of the ones that delivered the babies to the spiders so they could make them dirt babies. Sometimes mothers were not able to deliver their children as demanded them because their hearts were too heavy to do such a thing. The problem with the sojourn was that they were solitary, and the babies that were born, if a woman was lucky enough to find some semen. Problem was until the child was five they didn't become aware enough to operate their own sojourn. They were on their own. Before Breanna obtained her own sojourn she lived with her sisters as nomads in the past. Breanna and her sister Scarlet interacted with Amber through stealth dream sycronization to devise the dirt baby technology and delivery system. Amber didn't even realize the origin of her inspiration. A subset technology of advanced artificial intelligence that set on a path designed them. That same hardwire core of human brain that allows our species to survive (or a stranger to be kind to a stranger) is the same architecture used in the AI. An array of deceives and protocol so the little ones could thrive were developed.

The first time I met Breanna I thought it was just a dream. I was in a skyscraper being chased by a shadow apparition. I could not discern what it was on the roof. When I realized it was just a dream, I went to jump off the roof; she touched me and it felt serene but it was too late to recall my jump. I woke my body bouncing vigorously as my soul hit my body and stuck. My second encounter with her was a dream about my old house. As I sat on the back deck drinking coffee I looked out to see one of those children's play houses. A stuffed purple bear was leading a silent parade of a couple of stuffed Siamese cats and a walrus around the house. It was noiseless except for the sound of a baby crying. I saw her then; her hair was disheveled and bright red, her skin white with freckles, features small, dainty, and it all seemed dream distorted somehow. She was tall. I saw her placing babies in the field. They seemed to be pulled down in the soil by the spiders, so I called them dirt babies"

"Women want to have babies and not want to give them to the Troyons," Breanna stated, but I heard with my heart and head and not my ears. "The sojourns don't work with the babies; we need a way to hide them."

"It was a long time before I saw her again. I was afraid for her, thinking the Troyon's got her and all was comprised. I was then contacted by her in a vivid lucid dream that was more of a mindscape. My daughters told me she was never really there, they would always just go along with me. With all I was going through my fevers weren't worth the conflict. My overindulgence with enhancements allowed me to avoid any side-effects in everyone else's enhancements. Yet I remember sitting there conversing with her about the legion of Earthen spirits she would conjure to give my legion of fairies life, a soul, a consciousness. Problem was once the Troyon's were pushed back, they would counter with a scorched earth poison policy, and the dark energy reaction would be used to destroy the Earth and Troy. These Spirits in this form would be able to escape with humankind. The rachitic old wooden suspended bridge had three chains on each side for rails, a glow of a bright star, milky, behind heavy clouds, causing a fogdog, with dark stringy clouds passing in the foreground. The bridge led into the glow, disappearing in the distance. This path, though not the brightest, became the only path, and once stepping on the bridge it all accelerated."

"My one daughter Amber is good at spider applications. I will have her get on it immediately. But I need something from you. I need Ethereal Spirits to take forms. I am preparing to help mankind escape from this nightmare I need two hundred of them. I wondered why we were not communicating through the spider network and then realized we were, at a higher dream state. The goal was to manifest the physical realm of our adopted planet to the earth mass and energy to vanquish its enemies because they would poison it and kill us all and just move on to subjugate another planet. This energy need would cost the mass of the planet itself. I could not allow the spirits of this Earth to die, so I wanted them materialized so they could escape to their adopted world and no longer be terrorized."

Then there was that nightmare, shortly after Pete deployed the spider egg cases using crows, monk parrots and even large migratory birds to spread this technology as far as possible. Hope was then laid at the steps of the Sorority of the Ninth Fold. The dark energy network would have to be in place to accommodate the immense energy needed for the sojourn stealth technology. Pete was in a restaurant in Marina Towers. Looking up toward the street he saw twirling blue lights. The television crackled like a 1984 commercial. The anchor man looked both stoic and scared.

"The president of the United States has just been assassinated; the vice president has declared Martial Law until the Tea Party Terrorists and their military accomplices who have perpetrated this plot are brought to justice." Eyes darted around the tables, everyone trying to gauge everyone else's reaction. I checked my cell phone. It had no service, the network was dead. The government killed the network. I did the two-step finger man on my wrist and pointed to the river walk. My daughter Amber reacted immediately, jumping aghast on the news of the presidential assassination, pulling the table cloth and pulling coffee onto her dress.

"Oh! Stars and broomsticks daddy, I've soiled my dress. I'll be right back. I must go to the ladies room before the stain sets in." Amber's silk dress was the epiphany of covert camouflage. The fine fabric of Madagascar spider web made a beautiful dress when needed and now it was needed it was a prototype life suit that could be morphed to fit any occasion. Pete rose as his daughter stood and started off to the ladies room. "We'll go see the Chicago Stars when you get back honey!" Pete said as she left, which meant get your ass to the boat.

Pete sat and took out his cell phone. He pressed a button here and there and stood up as the bus boy brought fresh water to the table. He quickly made eye contact and mumbled how he was going out to try and get a signal, as the staff cleaned up the mess. Pete knew he wouldn't but he did not know who was paying attention. He heard sounds, a gnashing of talk and trouble. His cell phone began screeching audio feedback. Pete tossed it into the river. A thin young girl approached him.

"Lily says you will look after me!" Pete heard it through the spider device. They were on line. He grabbed the girl's hand and began walking with her. The spider reassured the girl as they walked. There were sounds of scrambling behind. Pete looked back, there was nothing; must be spider chatter, he thought. Pete wondered what Amber's location was and was immediately given information by spider that she was boarding the Chicago Star. As Pete hurried up the gang plank, child in tow, the mate gave the order. "Cast off!" The three of them went into the dining salon. A group of about fifty people were there, some sorting through the life suits on the table. Pete was baffled; he did not think that that many life suits were produced. Grabbing one Pete quickly donned it. The little girl's name was Wren, she already had a life suit on. As soon as Amber's prototype touched one of the new suits they just blended. The ship rocked violently. It ran up on something just as it left the break water.

"Abandon ship!" the announcement came over the public address system.

"All rabbits down your holes," Pete said as he made it to the deck. Other people were jumping in their life suit, covering them, allowing them viability in the cold Lake Michigan water. Just as the three jumped in a coast guard ship fired and hit the water line. That shock, that awakening into a new reality of the spider tech era made Pete's mind skip, it was already telling me that my wife was gone. "The more my mind felt confused because of the emotional toll, the Nano mites shifted me. This induced alexithymia state felt so unnatural, yet for this stage of the game it was thought necessary. Now that time has passed I wonder if I should try and recall the past."

"We swam for a while. The life suits adapted us to survive Lake Michigan waters. We were covered, warm, and had fins and breathe. We swam for the breakwater, but were redirected north along the lakefront by the spiders. They signaled us when we could go up for air. The cities were chaotic. We were given our sojourns but only wanted to use them if warned. We needed to get to the Milwaukee Port Authority.

Pete looked at Kyle, his eyes shedding tears. "I don't want to remember any more right now. Is that ok?"

Kyle reached over and shut off the recorder. "I'll go in and make some tea, give you a tick to get it together." Kyle said as he stoically stood and walked inside. Pete's mind indulged in crazed thinking.

Surely the Atomic Bomb is terribly sinister, but morally isn't it just as sinister to give us pistols to eradicate ourselves one at a time in a slow consuming agony? The introduction of chemical or biological warfare, whatever the death, it is the end of the world for those inflicted. No matter what the scourge, the right of self-preservation, even the arming ourselves with prophetic overkill, to arm ourselves to simply survive, it has been said it is better to have a gun and not need one than to need a gun and not have one. The scourge I shall apply to them will be of biblical proportions; they will be judged by the same measure pressed down; and I will deliver this blow decisively, for I am the grim reaper of Troyans. Memory and thinking put his brain in a whirlwind.

"I lay there in a fever as I looked down into the hall. The floor tiles became a landscape placing me in a vista. I was then in a fox hole at the end of the tiles, the pounding of the approaching giant footsteps woke me as again I lay in bed, each time falling into a feverish sleep, revisiting my dream reoccurring and waking countless times, until a nightmare of me into the flat where I grew up hiding under the bunk beds watching a fire encompass the room and a trap door opening and a round shoulder woman calling me to escape the nightmare. I climb though only to find myself in that fever soaked bed.

The Ark of the Covenant properly constructed generates energy: so you mean to tell me Earthen generated energy cannot be distributed to the human experience? I say you live in the falsehood of the realm you have constructed, afraid to embrace that alternate, fearful of your own change, that human experience so horrid that a leap of faith is the only escape. Do not be afraid! This child's hand I hold, this child Wren, she will become the center of my defense grid. I will implant optic fiber connections to her spinal cortex. I will cover these outlets with a symmetrical tattoo. All her hair will become fiber optic and coiled on her head in a smooth French braid, ready for connection.

The individual talent of the quality cog allows the machine of man to function. Therefore the existence of man will remain as long as the machine is allowed to work. Man's quandary is that of the depraved that prey on the weak allowing still others to oppress, and that he, man, one day may become that oppressive force he must purge from the society. The good people who do not rise up against tyranny are as much a part as a problem when they are the solution.

A vexing pondering is this connection of universes. Has this been used by man before to journey here from prior dying civilizations? The segment of mystery known as the Bermuda triangle, right next to it the land of Atlantis and Lemuria, connected through the Earth. There would be that rally point and the passage of civilization to civilization. To conceive a beginning traversing point to a starting point traveling through time in time, that dying civilization spawning another one. Through this portal the realm we are going to pass to cherished metal and technology, so we need to meld and mend our new home Phoenix."

Pete's eyes focused back to Kyle. He was gone: legal pad pages flipping back onto the pen and the pen skips away, clouds mass quickly, lightning plumes fill the sky, rich energy crackles through the dark matter network. Pete's life suit covered him completely. He picked up the Colt. He holstered it as it melted into his life suit. The lightning charged him to a ready state. Pete then realized this nightmare was not over. A cold wave shuttered Pete's body that turned to an outside shiver; he struggled to open his eyes. Then he saw her again, that witch that comes to him in his dreams, a relationship of helping each other help the cause. She began to speak to him.

"The basic faith of this Earth Witch is that she shares a cause with Mother Earth. That mission is to guard her children so they thrive and their actions to enhance the universal knowledge. The father who lives in Orion has put in motion a response to the unbalanced ways of the Troyon. The spirit of mankind and the spirit of Mother Earth shall inspire and guide man to rid him of this scourge. The spirits that are instilled in the earthen powers like wind, fire, earth and water, spirit of the breath of life, that essence at times of things one can't put their fingers on, the appearance of a dirt devil or a water spout or when your hair stands up on your neck, when a cool breeze shakes only one branch in an entire forest. The spirit of life locked away in chlorophyll. These are the spirits to take a physical presence to aid in man's thwarting of the Troyon oppression. The physically engineered fairies instilled with two hundred Earth born spirits.

The storm came tearing in fast and with plenty of lightning, constantly hitting and powering up his life suit. Kyle came running from the house, wind pelting him. Pete saw who Kyle was now. Kyle began to scream.

"You're a fucking loon!" Kyle yelled, laughing hysterically. "I should know, I am you." Then the storm seemed to just take him up in the sky. It was so windy Pete closed his eyes and he was there: the void, pre-big bang, he glimpsed it for that one tenth of , then Pete opened his eyes and saw his daughter Amber and she said.

"Ok dad, just relax and breathe deep. Kay, he's coming out of it. Give me a hand with him." Pete was lying in an epson fluid; he looked at them as if he didn't know them.

Kayla got under his shoulder and said, "Ok Dad, we're done with these enhancements now. You've gone far enough."

Four

⇾ WREN ⇽

"Any man who thinks he can be happy and prosperous by letting the Government take care of him better take a closer look at the America Indian." Henry Ford

Then there was the day the sirens all screamed, chatter reached the street that the president was assassinated, after all his promises, all his broken promises, that elusive utopia he had nailed down with the Troyon, his own quest for a legacy blinded him to the danger, which became horse blinders as he chose not to see the fiasco that flanked him. Wren took up temporary residence in the foyer of a shoe store front. A metal storm door had been pulled down it had a wrinkle, and Wren was thin enough to squeeze between the bars and the overhead door. Sneaking under and living on the tiles she pushed the broken glass away from the corner and put her bedding there. She always had to be careful of the shards of glass around her, but the glass gave her a sense of security, and the crunching was an early warning system.

The Public Address System just kept going, telling people what to do. Many surprisingly just listened. The leftover humanity became the vassals of war lords and street gangs that squeezed out the last of humanity from the shattered cities.

Radio Free America featured the voices of once great critics of the Troyans and their government alliance. Now their voices just dubbed bits of lies, spewing the government talking points, leading the followers to their demise. Does no one remember the principles they spoke of?

It was early morning and a different song came over the PA system, a song Wren remembered her mother listening to—"The Southern Cross," performed by Black Sabbath. Then the spiders came offering a new world of wonderous things. Wren seemed connected to the other surviving street kids, yet they kept their distance, so no organization could be seen. We were told things would get better as the power source increased output. As the spiders gave us stealth, our sojourns would follow, but first we learned how to hide in other deceptive spider ways, Wren hot-footed her step to keep up with other refugees. The streets strewn with the substrate of society look more like ghetto alleyways of debris, with death lining the curbs. The blood curdling screams seemed to finally cease. Wren was afraid, glances of motion fluttered in the streets as shy ghosts, as the sojourns were tested and dark energy conduits flooded with power. Wren's breath was knocked out of her as one of the human traitors grabbed her, pulled her into a doorway he smashed her up against a wall, she could smell the rot in his mouth.

She felt his hands grope her as he snarled, "Gunna get me a taste of you before I turn you over." She knew she had to hit him, and hard. Wren concentrated on her fist and struck. Her fist smashed into his skull and popped inside. She discovered her hand of hell! His head popped, sloshes of brain splashed all over; his eyes exploded, spraying Wren's face. She struggled to get her fist out of his skull. Wren shook the husk of a man off her arm, then she relaxed her hand, wincing in disbelief. Wren ran down the alley by the high rises through the clutter tossed streets. She heard a moaning she knew. Then there was a wailing, a baby crying, drawing its first breaths. The flotsam and jetsam of a once great civilization crunched under Wren's humble feet as she entered the building. The woman lay in the first small room inside, a shredded mattress next to her on the floor, a newborn on her chest.

"Take my baby and put her in the dirt. Please!" she begged. "They all lie, my baby is healthy," the mother's eyes plead in deep emotional tears. "We don't need laws governing bodies and babies' government just wants control over us." The mother crying, eyes welled soaking her face as she caressed her new born daughter and looked to Wren to save her child. Cloth, she thought as she pulled off a bit of sleeve from her life suit. Wren said nothing, just grabbed the child and held the cloth against her as the neo transmitter quieted her and Wren thought, enclose child newborn life suit. Wren directed her spiders to split, making two more spiders that spun enough fabric to complete the infant suit with the additional webbing from Wren's suit. The two cloned spiders tucked in the infant's soft skull, carrying the program of the newbie.

Wren knew that there was a park close by, and she knew she had to get the infant there. Wren had to put her in the grass by the swings. That was where the spiders would be able to take her and hide her, this would be the child's only chance. Wren could not take the infant to her sojourn with her. These babies, now known as dirt babies, would have to live in the earth with spiders and be cared for until they would be able to control their own sojourn. The webbing covered the babies, encasing them, putting them into spider-controlled stealth mode that would hide the baby.

Wren herself had to get to the river and then to the lake to be able to join up with the man and his daughter. They will be able to help her get out of the city. The city was no place to be a graveyard filled with a vast loathing from Earth bound spirits seeking revenge. Wren had to head out to the heartland. Fermi lab and Argonne labs became rallying points. Wren got to the park. She made her way to the swings and placed the baby down on the grass from all over the spiders came, covering the child, it almost seemed as if the earth swallowed her and all that was left was grass. Upon seeing this Wren had the realization that the world she had known and the society that she was once a part of from now on she was a new world, a world of oppression and cruelty, and she was in a society of stealth, the Sorority of the Ninth Fold.

Sirens scored the air with more wailing. The final move of the Troyon takeover went into effect, and therefore the major move of the sorority was in play. The sky rumbled in distant fireworks, a soft breeze brought a faint smell of almonds and apples. The cell network died, the internet vaporized, a static buzz filled the new network as it powered up to full capacity. Everyone with spiders' ears buzzed with the power up.

The snare was sprung and Wren's leg was caught. The life suit protected the anchor barb from setting itself in her ankle, but the snare was still tight, and the Troyon began to reel her in.

"Not so fast little one, you're mine, and now it's time for me to take mine," the Troyon overlord declared as he grabbed her ankle and lifted her to him, face to face. "A fresh morsel for me to consume," he said as he smelt her. He began drooling in revelry with his plaything. Wren's hell hand charged, she felt it get hard as hell. She swung as hard as she could. Catching the Troyon off guard he released her as he fell back on his bum. Wren concentrated on her hand. She told it that it had to be harder and strike harder still. The Troyon just looked at her his glimmering smile his heart warmed to find someone with some fight left in them. Wren took her best defensive stance. Her right arm from the elbow down to the tips in her fingers pulsed with an unknown energy.

The eerie smug laugh distracted him. She stood by the jungle gym. Gothic pale alabaster with long raven black hair, flowing satin and silk dress, eyes red but cold like space, yet the energy of stars deep inside. "You are as pathetic as the child you wish to devour," she taunted. She approached effortlessly toward the Troyon, capturing his gaze and attention he dismissed Wren and turned to her.

"You will writhe in pain having my child, if I don't split you in two first," the Troyon said in a bombastic voice. The closer she got the more spellbound he became. She got so close and went to kiss him. She sucked the life and lung out of the Troyon and merely let him fall. She spit his taste back onto his carcass and turned to Wren.

"Come little one," she said, holding out her hand. Wren was amazed wondering who she was. Her hand was calm now and turned to normal. She reached up and took Lilith's hand.

"Are you MKH?" Wren questioned taking her hand.

"Oh no my sister, I have been retained by your sorority for help in transition. My name is Lilith; you can call me Lilly, and your name is Wren?" Lilly said as she held Wren's hand in her hand and began walking with her. "I know your start has been very rough, but I have much to tell you before I must go, so as we walk I will talk." They seemed immune to the chaos around them as their sorority sisters sought sojourn, stealth and escape vanishing in the corners of the Troyon eyes. "Don't be concerned about the things around us Wren. Chaos is my element, and I must get you to your foster father quickly. That baby you hid was a sister, naturally conceived. These Troyon men have taken seed but they destroy the male bearing semen. Take no over lording from any men. Women are not their servants. We are equal, accept no other station. Our men are basically good and must be put in their place time to time, but again listen to their bravado and do it the way as you see fit. Troyon men are all just a murderous bunch and should be crushed mercilessly and completely. There is no other solution.

Your hand is your defense for now." Lilith stopped and squatted to rub the back of Wren's hand against her face. Lily's skin felt so cloud soft on Wren's hand, her eyes were so fiery red inside. Lilith's power must run deep, Wren thought. "This planet realm has now been open to a parallel foster planet. We will use this new realm's physics to survive and plan our reversal." Lilly began walking again. She was walking quickly, and she pointed to the man walking. "That is him. Go to him and grab his hand, your spider will announce you," Lilly said, lifting her arm up until Wren could no longer reach her hand. "Go!" Lilith said. "The power transfer is almost complete." Wren turned and Lilly was gone. She scurried and grabbed Pete's hand, looking up at him as they hurried toward the boat.

"We've got to hurry honey!" Pete said setting his grip in her hand. Wren heard him by word and she felt the words beginning to come through right to her brain, the spider network was connecting.

Amber was waiting on the vessel standing next to the hand rail, her body language outwardly shaken. Others got to the boat's gang planks, bowing with weight until the boat is cast off. As the Chicago Star ran a ground on the breakwaters everyone had donned their life suits. Not long after that a hovering ship appeared. Loud shots rang out. Everyone just jumped overboard their life suits on full survival. There was a blue pulse that hit the ship once in the water we realized more that this powering up of the spider grid gave a comfort in individual energy and capability. They all gathered together in clumps just below the water's surface headed toward the Milwaukee port authority. They were scared but strangely strong with this ethereal energy that permeated their suits. Soon they would be introduced to their sojourns where their enhancements and boosters would be completed. Then the transfer to the new realm would be irreversible.

Pete, Lori and Wren found themselves first on a Milwaukee beach and after stealth walking a bit then, onto the roof of the Gromann building. Amber was no longer with them but, Pete knew she was safe she just had a different mission. They opened their sojourns and stepped inside. That which they thought and needed were created and their thoughts were filtered informational communication to one another. Though they rested for three days awaiting a winged transfer to the Argonne, there was a buzz as the three exited their sojourns. Pete and Lori attached their sojourns to the long simple flying machine. Once Wren strapped herself in it would give a profile of a Blue Herron. As she jumped off the roof she felt the dark energy giving her light and insight. She saw the dying flames of an intense battle flicker like a dying candle, and then in a hurried burst of velocity several small craft shot like a bottle rocket disappearing in the night without a report.

Wren rethought her Heron broom to travel round the fading mayhem, she came low enough to jump on a treetop where spiders quickly secured her and her broom with the sojourns of Pete and Lori went off to hide in the Argonne forest facility. She hurried down to the injured solider. He was already engulfed in spiders as he was given a paralytic synapse block that stopped him from moving but he was aware of his surroundings. Stripping thin shavings of slippery elm the spiders massed them on Wren's palm. She then got close and pushed them into the hip wound of the solider it would form grist and help stabilize the hip. The spiders put manna webs out before dawn. Wren and the solider ate the manna that was collected. The following day the two were hidden in a tree all day in sojourns as Troyons scoured the area. On the third twilight when all was clear the Blue Heron Broom returned and Wren and Danny were taken to the Argonne.

The two touched down close to the meteorologist tower. A jump ship container pod revealed itself to them. It was hiding in Nano-camouflage. Wren helped the solider inside. Dim lights lit the area until they were inside and the doors closed. The lights then brightened to reveal a set of leather couches and a maze of gorilla glass spanning the entire area. Wren helped the solider down on the couch, a body harness with braids of optic fibers was set out on a stainless steel table. The spiders instructed Wren to enter the ominous looking harness, and told her that she was to be the nexus of communication between the remaining. Wren donned the harness. The optic interface tattooed

Wren's connection into her nervous system along her spine and arms. The connections were finished and the gorilla glass maze hummed with symbols, graphs and pictures. The braided optic fibers acted like a bungee, letting her hop and dance around to parts of the glass that need attention, integrating her optic nerves with swiping movements that coordinated the actions of the remaining of humankind strategic movements. A beautiful symmetrical artwork covered the optic fiber connections on Wren. Her hair a full hair tight smooth French braid, her connections spanned from her tail bone up to her neck.

Five

⇒ MARKED FOR DEATH ⇐

*The Father shall be known when he executech judgements: the
sinner hath be caught in the works of his own hands. Plasm 9 17*

The slim corridor led to the command suite of the elite Troyon
Earth command, the room containing computers and their
operators, Troyon guardsmen stationed at the doors.

"We are under siege, Seignior!" the operator announced.

The Seignior's chair spun around and he quickly ordered. "All
information crosses my screens. Close all hatches and entry-
ways." The commander's thoughts glistened a bit. Thousands of
years of plundering planets, sheer genius of conquest, like here
using their own media to deceive its masses as we systematically
brutalized them, each realization of malice explained away as
paranoia of a reactionary few, not the free-spirited goodness of
the collective.

The Seignior studied the film clips and information coming to
his desk. Nazis or Necromongers or whatever the name of evil
before them, it is just jaw dropping the vulgar work that can be
created by evil when it is left unchecked. His stone cold black

heart felt just a pulse of fear which was quickly extinguished by his arrogance, but his eyes did not lie, he reluctantly gave his next order.

"All guardsmen strip all the flesh from behind all females' ears. Then begin immediate boarding for immediate departure." The Seignior grabbed his weapon and ran for the departure area. The Troyon guardsmen acted, cries rang out from the girls. Those late night whispers and unsettling dreams of the Troyon all revealed as true by this action, shucking the flesh from behind the ears, not mattering if it took an ear or two.

The girls in several attempts rushed the guard, trying to go toward the turmoil but were stopped, herded back to the ship. Still alive only because of the value the Troyon had for them.

Six

☞ BODY GUARDS ☜
(THE GRIFFINS)

In wartime, truth is so precious that she should always be attend-
ed to by a bodyguard (of lies). Winston Churchill

T he quarter moon was off the horizon. It was light enough
to walk by. Rocket was curdled up against Brea's neck in
a deep fairy sleep. Breanna carried her adopted Blue
Heron broom, her halo and all her magic that defined her
combined to help guide her. Her witch's halo seemed to pulse
and bring her energy and vision; it was much more helpful than
she would have ever thought and along with her emotions the
hues in hair changed their shades of red. Brea only liked riding
her Blue Heron broom for night flights, but tonight someone
needed to spread her wings. Breanna took her finger and gently
rubbed Rocket.

"Hey, get up you, time to eat and get some wing time little
one. I need you to take a look around." Rocket stretched. She
could feel herself grow when she did that, but she was always so
hungry. Brea anticipated that and handed her a chunk of chooga

cake. Chooga cake was better, Rocket thought, when it has cinnamon in it. "Rocket, when you finish up, I need you to get a little altitude and get a look about okay?" Brea asked as she took out a blatter of water and took a drink. Breanna turned the canteen in the air until a bit of water came to the nozzle. Rocket hovered there, drinking water to wash down her cake.

Rocket flew up, getting a look around. A sharp putrid smell bit her nose, brought her cake up to the bottom of her throat.

The stench seemed to be coming from the west in a light breeze. The smell just wrapped around oneself. Rocket quickly flew down and whispered in Brea's ear. "Smells like death that way." Rocket simply pointed, Brea arched her hand in a C shape so Rocket could sit, her legs still growing stronger but now mostly shin bone with still forming feet that she used as a rudder when she flew, too delicate to stand on for now.

"Here Rocket, take this and put it behind your ear. We'll be able to talk to each other, and the network will be able to get an exact location." Breanna's finger held a small spider. It was a small spider mite so they would have input in the network AI. The spider took its place behind her ear and kept on a thick filter. Because of the fairy privacy, their elusiveness aided their accomplishments. "Next time I'll put cinnamon in the chooga cake." Breanna simply smiled.

As they walked westward it wasn't long before the Earth beneath Brea's feet began smelling of death. Rain and weather washed and blew the stench further from the origin, bleeding into the soil and air. Then they saw the field of corpses that stretched as far as the eye could see, leftovers of a gluttonous race whose prodigy did not even have the decency of finishing its first meal. The death of all these women, the sight and smell of them, cast fear and doubt into Breanna and Rocket. She sat on the edge of that field of decaying corpses, each arrival of half eaten corpses having different rates of decay. The latest still had the horror engraved on their faces, the older remains somehow finding an eerie contentment in their common suffering, weathering skeleton smiles and leathery patches of flesh mourning a violent self-defeating death. The dark scene was visually a snapshot of a most atrabilious time of humankind.

The raucous cry of a crow momentarily snapped the girls from their melancholy. Rocket flew to Brea's neck, so their touch would console each other. Breanna walked to the edge of the fallen, her hair turning fiery red, her witch's halo pulsing. Gems sparking power, she raised her crystal toped scepter. "I thank you Father for these tools for without them these sights would have devastated me. Mighty Father in Heaven, I implore you to grant me a visit with your Wisest Solomon, for I seek an army of demons to champion me and my sister so we may escape our unholy scourge. That gift of procreation given to us by the Father since the time of Lilith, has been corrupted by this unholy league, grant us the gifts we need to defeat our enemies.

Father of Heaven, hear and heed this Mother's cry, we are in need of your divine intervention." Breanna prayed, invoking and conjuring until a swirling breeze took hold, turning and spinning faster and harder until a portal opened. From this a white bearded man crowned and adorned, perched on his green carpet, he stands off his throne his body guards fierce soldiers of the Sphinx. His carpet hovers in front of Breanna and Rocket; his voice moves the air in a powerful way.

"I am here as an answer to a prayer. Breanna, what do you wish me to do?" Solomon asked very perplexed.

"I need to rescue my sisters and an army enslaves our people. I need a legion of demons to march on my enemies and a portal to save my sister. I ask you this O wise Solomon, as I am at an impasse. Look at their horrid ways," Brea asked in humility and all earnest, waving her hand over the scene of decimation.

"A legion, you do not need a legion. Humankind has already been seasoned for war. Listen in the stillness for the spirit voice of inspiration, mankind will vanquish their oppressors. Your sisters are a different problem. Two demon architects that constructed the portal system for my temple, that I use even now, shall help reunite you with your sisters and act as your personal bodyguard until they are no longer needed." Solomon handed Brea a ring with a six pointed star. "Wearing this ring will give your voice command over these demons. I will give them their mission and you will use the ring to mold your needs. Their names are Hermes and Hector. From this point forward you and your sisters will be known as 'Soloman Witches'. With the last word reverberating in the air, a wind came up so fast their eyes just closed until all the dust blew away. The light was so bright they kept their eyes closed and covered with their hands. A short time passed and all seemed calm except for wings pounding air. Looking up Brea and Rocket saw Hermes and Hector in all their regalia. Wings beautifully designed and highlighted with horns and chain male feathers, the scaly head and shoulders of a dragon with the bill of a Russian Sea Eagle, front legs like a Komodo dragon, torso of a lion, rear legs of a black spotted leopard, and the three-pronged spaded tail of a Snally Gasior. Rocket's wings just unfurrow, tilting, her wings taking the downdraft up from the powerful hovering slipstream of the pair of bodyguards, going eye to eye with the Griffin. Rocket bent her body at a ninety degree angle at her hips, her wings steady gliding on air, and she looked in his eyes, nose to nose looking into Hector's teal lizard eyes. Closer and closer Rocket peered in his eyes, and then she spoke.

"You have very pretty eyes!" Rocket stated. This disarmed Hector, and tipped him a bit back on his spiked heels: no fear and this fairy has no fear. Hector's scattered speckled eyes staring into Rocket's azure pools, there is a connection here.

Then in an instant the two demons were eight foot tall, heavy armored and spiked winged soldiers with formidable battle axes. Then they were men, cloaked and hooded, caramel colored skin with those same teal lizard eyes. Pulling their hoods back, they were bald, faces with a no nonsense air. Hermes approached Breanna and spoke.

"Hail Sister, my brother will make haste to retrieve your sister and return her. Hector will leave now from here and we shall pick them up at the cemetery." Hector approached the pair, and spoke briefly.

"I will return swiftly with your sisters, and you Rocket, your hundred and ninety-nine sisters are already being born awaiting your insight." Hector raised his wings, morphing into his full demonic self, and shot toward the sky, melting to nothing against the blue as a bright flash flickered on the border of a blue world.

Rocket flew to Hermes. "I don't know who your brother is trying to impress, but I am faster you know!" she said thoroughly impressed and not willing to show it.

"Good!" Hermes said, seeing the vanity in this one. "You will need to be faster than Hector to be able to complete your mission." Breanna became whiter and whiter, her energy draining as the labor of life started for the fairies. "Take her Heron broom little one, it will help you find Kayla. She is the one who has set up this nursery. Find her and take her to the birth place. I will fly Breanna to the portal to meet her sisters, she will have more energy when she joins them. Hermes grabbed her as she swooned down, grabbed her and morphed into a griffin flying away. Rocket flew using that broom saving her strength to help her finish the birthing.

Hermes and Breanna landed. Brea, feeling better, stood out in the clear night. The stars looked so cold and distant in the low pre-dawn light, their breath was the only fog on that crystal night, and the moon was a quarter; waxing toward the hunter's moon. These tools they were seeking were hidden on holy ground in a cemetery. Their attention was given to a large shrine, an angel who was in the center of the veterans' section. Hermes came up to the statue and grabbed its hand as if to shake it. He used his strength as he squeezed the granite hand until it slightly crumbled revealing an embossed piece of metal with a set of numbers on it; they poked and prodded the ground among the headstones to find a marker with the lot and block of fifteen and fifty-four. The grave marker was a simple bronze plaque; Peter Xenon U.S. Army Special Operations. Once they found their location Hermes then donned his demon self and began to dig.

Hermes dug to the burial vault. He pulled the cover off the vault, exposing a beautiful mahogany casket. Seven metal tridents struck deep into the wood.

"These are the signs of great warriors," Brea said, fear resonating in her voice. "We should not disturb things further. We need to put this back before these powerful souls seek retribution, Hermes."

Hermes inhaled deep, smelling the casket. "No, my witch, no decaying flesh rests here. It is but a ruse."

"It may well be a deceit but we still must respect these signs. Hermes, help me pluck the tridents. I will put them in my witches' pouch to store them until I find these warriors and tell them of their great deed." Brea pinned the tridents in her pouch in a most high place of reverence. Later Brea wove one of them into her braided halo of gems and hair as a reminder of the quest to return these showing her gratitude to the soldiers who left these tools for her.

Removing the seventh trident opened the casket revealing the three crystal staffs Breanna and Hermes would use to bridge the corridors of time, so the sisters would be able to pass to this time. The casket was made of African mahogany. Three staffs ran parallel to one another. On each side inside rings which were used to carry the casket, one across the top laced and woven through the top cover. Breanna removed the dirt from the locking slot and pushed in the embossed metal tag and turned it. The staffs released. Hermes then removed the staffs alongside the open front of the casket and found a diamond, ruby and amethyst. A white marble altar stood in the center of the cemetery.

A monument closest to the area had seven granite steps with a granite angel standing on the top stair holding a sword upward depicting the stairway to heaven. Brea placed the crystal topped staffs in three designated holes on the stairs making a light rail; the sky began crackling in energy.

The grey granite angel was wielding a sword, guarding the stairway. Hermes walked up to the angel and morphed to the opposite of it, the Griffin that he was. He wrapped his hands around the stone angel's hand. Holding the sword together; the angel became supple and moved enough to form an arms bridge with a sword peak on the top step. The air charged more. Brea stood on the bottom of the stair. She held her sister's halo in front of her as if she was placing it on her sister.

Fifteen ninety-two and the two witches stood next to the demon. They entered the portal Hector possessed a small amount of plasma, a gift forged of the spirits of universe for they too had a future in this. Their realm would not die and end this gene pool. The planet of destination is a planet waiting to be sown the seeds of humanity. This world is inviting them as a mature species. Scarlet and Naomi passed through the portal. Hector was last, grabbing his Brother Hermes' uplifted arm and closing the portal. The light to close the portal was so heavenly bright one could see through their own hands as they covered their eyes they all made haste before the Troyon would investigate.

The Pelican landed so gently, it was as if it were a breeze. A father and son Troyon hunters were tucked in the ridge side; they were overlooked. The father grabbed the son's shoulder and squeezed it as a sign of success. Wren sat in the luxury suite module of the Pelican as Lori entered from the flying frame.

"So, we're here to pick up the plasma?" Wren asked, her mind and body recovering from the onslaught of more interface connections, her back and the back of her arms covered with a beautiful tapestry of connections that looked like an intricate tattoo.

"Rest here my sister, I shall be back quickly. The plasma is an energized material that should be able to pierce the armor of the Troyon," Lori said without reservation. Lori hugged her sister as she sheathed her samurai sword across her back and opened the gangplank and exited. The mission foremost on her mind with the comfort of darkness put Lori at an ease the Troyon took advantage of.

Lori moved quickly through the Missouri woods to the entryway into the cavern. She went to the pool just inside and dove in the water going deep and coming back up on the other side of the cavern in its interior. Hector and Hermes stood in their armor, Scarlet and Naomi lay sleeping, Breanna stood looking at Lori pulling her hair back and squeezing the water from it, they all looked haggard and drained. The griffins stood steadfast with their battle axes ever vigilant.

"Are you the witches my uncle speaks of?" Lori asked, now seeing and believing, thinking before that it was just the rants of an old over-medicated man. The red hair witches and body guards were no illusion.

"Yes, yes we are witches of whom your Uncles speak," Breanna answered. "We will talk at another time but now time is of the essence. Surrender your sword to Hermes my protector and he shall sharpen it against his talon, which will inoculate it with plasma. The plasma will multiply by using the flesh of the Troyon as you slice them open," Brea explained as Hermes stepped forward. Lori took her sword and handed it to Hermes handle first. He took the sword and ran the blade across the edge of his talon, infusing Lori's Samurai with the plasma. As Hermes handed back the sword Hermes came close and spoke softly in her ear. His whisper sent an ice water bath up Lori's spine, and the focus of the message even more fearful.

"Wren is in imminent danger. Run, she has been discovered."

The strings of life that Lori was rebuilding were about to be strummed another chord. Those paralyzing fears of many of her lost friends and relatives began to bleed out from those hidden places deep within.

"Save her!" Breanna yelled, imploring to the momentarily frozen Lori. Brea's light mystical touch released her trance as she bolted and dove into the pool.

Wren's vision focused in and out as she dozed on the round center couch in the middle of the commons. Then the pain came, so hard of a punch it knocked her to the floor.

"Oh hoh, the little girl woke up," the Troyon father said as he kicked Wren in the ribs. His son stood off to the side grinning, loving his father's actions. He tossed Wren back on the couch and approached her. When the Troyon got close enough, she felt his breath as she closed her eyes to concentrate on her fist of hell and struck. The Troyon went flying across the room but was unhurt because of his shell.

"Look at that Dad, a spunky one," his son said egging on his father. "You're not going to let her get away with that are you?" The father and Wren traded multiple blows, trashing the room, the son looking on in glee. Wren's hand of hell only threw him across the room it couldn't penetrate the armor.

Lori was moving so fast, yet she saw herself in slow motion. The leaved whips of the underbrush lashed her skin, welting it because of her speed. All of a sudden the spider's alert went red. The Pelican had been breached and communication had somehow been suppressed. Lori leaped; it seemed to take so long.

Wren got thrown on the couch. She felt like a rag doll. Her hand of hell diminished her spider network. Shut down to avoid further detection, she lay there, sweat and blood blurring her vision.

"That's my girl, you just lay there. I'll take care of the rest." The Troyon stripped off her pants and dropped his own Wren was helpless and afraid. The Troyon pushed up against her knees and stepped toward her. Wren looked through, tears, blood and sweat. She felt his body shudder that such a changing of events, then nothing. The Troyon father, his facial expression one of disbelief, then green vomit flowing, started slowly then increased, his arm began reaching up, but stopped, and fell to his sides. He collapsed, becoming a mass of green plasma. Standing there was Lori, starring at her blade. It killed a Troyon. She was amazed, and standing there flabbergasted she heard the boy cackling.

"What happened was just a glitch. We need to get hold of the transition team, and this was all just a mistake." Lori approached the boy, the sword in front of her. The spiders routed around the damping field.

71

"Now just put that sword down. I have already changed my harmonics on my shield, it will not work again."

Lori's steely eyes told him his rant was in vain, her heart a cold stone to his plight. Closer and closer she moved toward him, slightly grinning as she thrust her new blade into his abdomen. The Troyon boy's eyes shone dying fear as the plasma from his father channeled through and destroyed him into a puddle of plasma.

"Don't fuck with my sister!" Lori said as she turned her blade and to her sister Wren. Lori cradled Wren and pulled her up to a sitting position. Wren was stirring back to a more conscious level. "Hey, baby girl, you doing ok?" Wren just wrapped her arms around Lori and tried to hug her. "I figure we got about seventy-two hours before shit hits the fan."

The Pelican touched down on the tarmac next to the stealth hanger. The two Uncles Mike and Pete walked over to the stairs of the Pelican. Pete put his arm out and took Wren from Lori.

"She needs to go to her control module," Lori stated. They all went to her nexus module. They laid her down on her bed, the spiders tending to her.

"So, what were you thinking?" Mike said with a stern look on his face.

"I may have broken mission protocol, but I have the plasma," Lori announced.

"Well that's a horse of another color," Pete said doing his best '*Wizard of Oz*' doorman voice.

"We need to get that plasma integrated into the snake fighters and get some to the military. The clock is now ticking," Mike said, his eyes getting lost in internal thought. "Got no time, let's get rigged and get going, no time." Mike knew the plan would have to come together. The two uncles left in their snake fighters to bring the plasma to the military offensive soon to begin.

$\mathcal{S}$even

➤ BIRTH OF A FAIRY ❧

Imagination is more important than knowledge – Albert Einstein

Breanna, when she was hidden in history, was taken out of her time and placed under an earlier set of stars therefore her magic was less effective. Living in the present time she is much more effective and can feel the aligning energy run through her and could not wait until her sisters got there to affect their power triangle. She didn't know how her lost sisters would be found but she felt it as a self-determined fact of feeling. Brea knew that morning it was time for her to begin her quest. She set off to find that birthing place of the fairies. Brea promised Pete she would instill spirits into the conscience of fairy flesh, a masterpiece of procreation.

The guard rail on the exit ramp was pitted and worn from time; cracks in the asphalt were full of prairie flora. A green sign with white words "Veterans Parkway" stood under the ribbon of clover leaf road that was crumbling under the weight of Troyon era erosion. Brea wore her witch's halo over her red braided hair. She had her most powerful scepter hanging from a rope spun of witch blown spider web, a worn deck of Rider Waite Tarot cards, and a half scorched Pecan Handled broom that fell in front of her on a windy day as she walked under a tree—Brea thought of it as a gift from her sister Scarlet, and for some silly reason believed she might need it someday—and a White Birch Wand with a clear Quartz top. Brea's hand reached deep down in her new cloak's pocket. Her finger felt the tip of a stone. She pulled it from her pocket and looked. It was a rune stone, the letter R Raidho: she was about to embark on a physical journey that would aid in the healing of her soul. Brea started walking north seeking this spiritual birth place. She went on her pilgrimage to call on the Father to implore two hundred Earthen Spirits to take physical forms to aid mankind.

Breanna had a waking dream. She heard the caws of the crows high in the treetops before the evening Sun. 'OZ we go' it instructed. She took the evening to get her bearings and traveled at night at first. It was more treacherous yet safer in a strange play on the way and the day. Breezy traveled light. Out of her sojourn she slept outside as much as possible, relying on the spiders to alert her to the Troyon hunting parties. Breanna just loved being so close to the things of the Earth. They loved each other so, and for the Earth it will give its existence for all Earth's species one day. The realms of Angels, Fairies and witches have been sucked dry by man's logical mind and cast aside. These entities live in that thin line of universal time that is dimensionally infinite. Those spirits tied to this Earth will be invited to take form and flee with their Earthly co-inhabitants with the help of the physics of the new home; this New World physics already started working in this World Realm. The Troyon sent out hunting parties periodically to search for these Earth-bound people, there has been no human seen outside the propagation prisons since the big purge, a kind of final disrespect to the species. Troyons thought mankind became a metaphysical entity. Very few were close to the concept that this shadow world existed. Then Brea saw the sign. It read 'Oswego' with a capital Z written over the S (OZwego).

The pale August blue moon hung mystically low on the polarized lite horizon. The pond was long, dark and ever so still, a mirror capturing the pictured landscape—a healthy tree lined shadow in a scattered cirrus sky. The air was sticky as a faint summer breeze fluttered the face of the moon moth wings. Its sublime glow seemed to light a secret path, its shimmering iridescence. Brea was told those girls hid things there. These girls were stealthy; they had to be to survive.

Breanna would rely on her guide Aster to help with the incantation to have the spirits take on fairy flesh. Breanna sky clad, her milky white skin aglow, matching the moonlight; she swept the area with her charred broom handle chanting a cleaning spell. "Sweep clean sweep clean." Brea poured a ring of salt and sat in the middle, her wand in front of her gaze and voice lifted upward, commanding, "Father in heaven your daughters are under siege, we pray to you. This world this Mother Earth will be destroyed by these invaders, oh heavenly Father we need two hundred Earthen Spirits to fill the flesh of fairies to help us drive these invaders out and spare your loyal spirits." Breanna then stood scepter in one hand wand in the other, arms outstretched to the heavens. Breanna completed her plea. "Father even the sparrow of the field does not fall unless you allow it, I plea with you for this divine help. Mother, oh Mother conjure us up a fairy Queen of cups so she may drink from the trough of life and have many offspring. Mother implore our Father to allow us what we need, for with divine intervention your Father by our side in this intelligent design we will survive." Brea's shoulders fell; voices brushed her ears, spirit breath breezes. She donned her new hooded cloak vestment. Its color changed to whatever was necessary; it was made of the same material as the life suit and Brea walked back to the house, close to the water filtration plant where she hid. She wanted to know more about those who lived there.

The large Erlenmeyer flask began to stir. It was on the shelf above the cluttered desk. Two optic fiber leads were connected to it and another 199 glass containers, flasks and up to five gallon water cooler bottles. Black Jacks, Brea's familiar cat was attracted to the stirrings of the Erlenmeyer flask. As the Earthen Spirits passed by to see how they would take part in this episode, Black Jacks jumped up by the flask and walked by it hard. It slightly teetered and spun quickly. Brea felt the spirits travel through as goosebumps trickled down her spine. The flask fell and broke and Black Jacks saw that Rochelle was a little premature. From the shadows Twitch the Bengal cat ran over and began sniffing enthusiastically, segments of its coat twitching as its tail furiously shook and bent. Twitching uncontrollably, he pawed at her and sniffed, being a curious cat. Pawing so vigorously the fairy drew it first breath, a spirit drew into its lungs awaking the flesh. Rochelle was her name, also known as Rocket.

Right now she was a sopping bunched up winged lump. Her wings were that of a swift swallow yet platinum white, her eyes cobalt blue. Her slight body needed to grow into those beautiful wonderful wings. Her ears large, but that would not last long, for once she started to fly and achieve her speed the flesh would be burned back becoming an exude point for plasma fuel as her hair was used for fuel storage, and like a dolphin slipping out of the outer cells to get a quick getaway this fairy was fuel and fire of wing. Rocket's hair was a straight platinum blonde. Her vanity always tried to have her hair long enough to cover the ear holes once they burnt off. Rocket would never ever slow down enough for her ears to ever grow back anyway. When she reached top wing speed her hair shattered a bit here and there and would produce a fairy dust that, catalyzing with the wing wind (contrails), would push Rocket to mind boggling speeds.

It was a large brick house about half a mile from the water distribution plant. What Brea liked best was a top observation deck. The deck gave a good view of the surrounding area. Brea would set up her sojourn there so she could have the high ground. She felt a little safer when she could see what was coming and she had to keep an eye on the sky for signs. The people that had lived there were older. By the pictures they had grown children. They never returned to the house but a cellar unveiled a cache of survival foods and other survival gear.

A kaleidoscope of dawn's colors pushed up from the horizon. Low hanging clouds make a false horizon—the Sun's light prismatic properties diffused the coming light until light again flooded the darkness. Brea kneaded the ration bag meal; oat meal with brown sugar sounded tasty. She squeezed the bag as she walked to the domed filtration plant. Her spiders opened the doorway in as she entered and began walking to her station. She heard the dripping onto the floor from the broken flask. Breanna's eyes looked down trying to figure what happened as a crunching of glass met her step. Her eyes followed the cascading drip from the shelf to desk to floor. A curled swift winged fairy lay on the floor amidst the broken glass and fluids. Breanna stepped over some broken glass. She bent down and scooped up some of the fluid. She began blowing on it. A fabric formed. It blew in the air. She turned and twisted her hands making fine veils of a platinum fabric-liquid platinum, mercury-nickel-cobalt and copper forged with the dark energy in this earthen witch's breath as she placed them on Rocket. Brea picked her up-carefully. The fairy's breathe shallow and labored, she placed her under a large glass container with an oxygen hose. A wooing tone hit the glass. It pleasantly vibrated; Brea could only think it to be a coo of contentment. "Black Jack-Twitch what went on here?" Brea questioned sternly. Twitch quickly bounded on to the table. He was a Bengal Hybrid and Brea's familiar.

Brea studied her as Rocket lay there, her breathing getting more stable. Brea reached under the glass with more blown fabric. Brea made sure the dome was vented properly, covered the fairy and went about looking for that Enfamil the former inhabitants had stashed in the sub cellar.

Breanna fed her the formula a few days until she was ready to come out from under the oxygen tent. Brea prayed, cared for Rocket and checked the setting on the other incubators. Rocket would snuggle in against Brea's neck as Brea busied herself readying her instructions on monitoring the embryonic fairies. Rocket, Twitch and Black Jacks became an odd trio of kindred spirits, their curiosity always seeming to lead to high-jinx.

Eight

❯ SCAVENGER HUNT ❮

"Here kitty kitty kitty."

Rocket and the two witches' feline familiars, Black Jacks and Twitch, would rummage around the ruins and look for the best things to reclaim, bringing back samples and directing others where stashes of goods and materials are located, in their version of a scavenger hunt. The Troyons were attracted to the movements of Rocket, as they were to the strange power fluxes with opening of Sojourns, thinking they were a ghostly gateway, so the Troyons would go on their ghost hunts, seeking to curb any energy that could affect them negatively.

Comet was named after the Comet class of fairy 'Comet' herself. She was fast. Rocket and Comet were only separated by hundredths of a second, like the difference between silver and gold in the Olympics. Comet flew higher recon; Twitch was sniffing around the back of the stove. His hind quarter had a spasm, and he didn't feel comfortable in back of the stove and started to back out when snap! The slap clap trap was built to maim. If it wasn't for his flexible bone structure Twitch's injury would have been graver, yet he cried out in a long moaning roll, then an array of cries and whines. Twitch's vocalizations screamed trap, but that 'trap' was Rocket's dilemma. She had to figure out how to get Twitch free and not get caught.

Rocket took the challenge of being caught that would be the only way to figure a resolution. Comet came in lower over the building to direct assets in place, as in the technology of the stealth fairy; all fairies are elementally quick, and Comet and Rocket's speed became legendary, as their elemental spirits of wind were casted to fifty fairies, as fifty for the each of remaining signs, Fire, Water, and Earth. These four Earth signs corresponded with the four suits of the tarot, swords, pentacles, cups, and staffs. The fairy is the ultimate optical illusionist. It thrives not only by its speed but the sound it makes with its wings; this sound enters the brain of all entities human or alien. The harmonic chirp impacts the entity at that 1/10 of a second time lapse perception in one's own eye to brain connection and can make it either seen or unseen or take on an appearance of a bird, butterfly or bat.

Rocket went down the rear stairwell into the hall that leads to the kitchen; she popped inside as the doors slammed shut. A strobe light spattered the walls as the different types of recorders tried to capture the true image of Rocket. A few copper wire surface protectors and a copper tea kettle gave her an idea. Rocket picked up a small piece of copper and accelerated toward Twitch. She quickly stopped and pushed the metal forward, which took the energy and went hot molten, which then melted the hinge assembly of the trap. Rocket again accelerated with a copper surface protector toward the door. As she released the metal the energy transfer to the copper, it blew an excited ultra-hot mass through the door.

The two Troyons on the other side of the door were splattered by the hot metal but their exoskeleton armor stayed impervious. They positioned themselves outward slightly so as not to get in each other's crossfire. The next thing out that hole in the door would be subjected to a hail of weapons fire. Rocket jetted out the opening, a drop of molten metal fell across her cheek and neck; she began rolling to be missed by the weapons fire but also to roll off the pain, but that drop of molten metal that hit her did more: its heat with her acceleration caused a cool light burst that entered the Troyon optical-to-brain highway and overloaded their visual sense, stunning them except for a wild stream of weapons fire as Twitch emerged from the hole screaming a gut wrenching piercing cry, adding to the Troyon disorientation. They were startled, breathing heavy as both Troyons sneezed simultaneously. Unbeknownst to the Troyon hunters the room they were in was full of cats that Black Jack had led there. The allergens of the cats themselves and the dusting up in the room irritated the Troyon airways as they began coughing sneezing and wheezing. With watery eyes and already unclear vision they stumbled out vacating the room and the corridors. The other Troyon back-up teams were in the same situation, partially blind, piercing headaches, and breathlessness.

Out in the open Rocket's air-fairy sisters swarmed her as a flock. They moved back and forth in unison as a united front, taking on the look of a flock of starlings. The flock moved to the Argonne. Rocket's cheek and neck were stinging. Rocket left her sisters entering the air tube to the Argonne corridor. She began feeling flush as shock started to wear in and she began weakening because of the large amount of energy expended in her flight.

Pete was startled. Rocket appeared against his neck. As he reached for her she tumbled into his hand unconscious. He saw her burn and carried her to an exam table, softly talking to her.

"It'll be okay honey, I'll fix you, it's worse than it looks." As Pete looked over her neck with his magnifier he saw the molten alloys bonded with her platinum physique. As he looked up he saw Tori, a fire fairy of empathy and Kimberly an Earth fairy, a natural healer. Tori's alabaster complexion cuddled up against Rocket, her pink ridged sensitive ears melding with Rocket; she reached out to Kim and held her hand, using that connection to relay Rocket's condition. Kim's wings had two sets, an upper and lower set. A lavender hue started with her wings and enveloped all of her, slowly engulfing the three fairies.

"Pete you must help my sister, the spider technology cannot fix her. What is wrong with her?" Kim said turning to Pete with a dumbfounded face. Pete stroked and pulled hard on his chin.

"It is serious Kim." Tori pulled aback aghast, afraid for her. Pete's eyes looked down and cupped Rocket's head. "See here," as he pointed toward her neck. "When she hit the molten metal it caused an acceleration pulse the metal forged at such a high temperature it caused cool light blast, a flash so intense, the need for heat pulls the heat from the surrounding area, dropping the temperature at least thirty degrees. I can fix it, but she has a fluid body mass if she gets weak or after a fast run. It will take a while before the patch realigns itself so the scar will be visible and the pain will reoccur. Rocket will get very weak until the spider patch can realign itself and return things to normal."

Tori shuddered inside. She knew Rocket had a delicate self-esteem. She was so proud of her beautiful face behind all that speed and it gave her a confidence.

The door opened by half and Casey flew in. She was red haired, with a kind off greenish hue on her snug clothes. Her wings were twin arches, brown sugar brown with a bailing, a type of batfish look. Casey's forearm gauntlet came almost to her elbow. She held a case and handed it to Kim. "These are skin fabric Pete told me to get from the lab." Casey looked into Kim's eyes, "We're going have to reconfigure this. We'll have to go over the exit strategy plans later when you finish, so when you're done here check in with the Queen of Swords." Kim nodded. Racheal the Queen of Swords was very stern uncompromising fairy. At times it was hard to defend a position with her.

Pete gently covered her wound with the skin and placed a bell jar over her and poured a nutritious liquid on her bedding that would be taken up into body. Three loud echoing booms filled the halls of the facility, followed by three more. Amber was at her station computing figures; she changed her monitor to camera and saw a hooded figure carrying a bundled blanket. Amber asked her dad what to do. He looked at the monitor.

"She is a Solomon Witch, an ally of mine. Her name is Breanna. I am busy with an emergency now, you will have to meet with her and see to her needs," Pete said and cut communication with her. Amber called to her sister Kayla to help her with the witch. The sisters went to the main entrance and opened the heavy door. Brea came in as soon as the door was opened enough.

"About time you opened that door." She handed Kayla the bundle. "The spiders can't fix my familiar so I brought him here. I need you to fix him; he was foraging for your father." Several blue balls swirled around the room. Kayla placed the bundle on a table in the isolation room. As she pulled back the sheet she heard a whining feline: it was Twitch.

"We must check that energy connection, still have rogue energy balls floating about," Amber said in a matter of fact way. Brea pulled back her hood and pulled the tie of her cloak, pulling it off and casting it to the wall where it stuck like Velcro. Her hair was a fiery red adorned by her witch's halo. Brea's hair became fiery red. Because of her intense emotional state her halo glowed in power.

"Maybe they are just your father's fairies keeping an eye on you," Brea said knowingly, "Now! Can you fix my cat?" she reiterated forcefully.

Amber and Kayla looked at the cat. It grumbled in a low growl. Its fur was a hard mess: the heat had singed the top in a matted crust. A closer examination showed strips of once molten metal seared into the flesh of the animal, the bonding causing a painful cohesion. The girls pulled back the fur, the metal bonded to the shoulder bone. When Rocket spun to maneuver in her escape some molten fairy flesh metal got in the mix, and that flesh also bonded to Twitch's flesh. The second eyelid was closed when that white hot piece of liquid burned what looked like a claw mark forehead to chin. (Twitch's fur eventually grew back, a platinum alloy fur, leaving a silver streak across the eye, shoulder to back with a touch on the tail.) They shaved the matted hair to get a better look at his injuries. Kayla and Amber forgot Brea was in the room, but Breanna turned away from the wall. A stainless steel case just seemed to be there and she opened it. She showed Kayla and Amber. It was a very small amount of liquid skin for burns, but it was for fairies.

"Your Father says I must put this on the burn," Brea said calmly. "The fairies brought it from your father."

"We'll have to fine spray it to have coverage," Amber said.

"Oh no! I'll put it on!" Brea said with a knowing attitude in her voice. She dipped one finger nail in then the other as the container sat on the table. She began to lightly blow as the liquid began stretching and thinning out a floating piece of fabric. She looked intently, turning her hands slightly this way and that until she was over Twitch, then in the blink of an eye the bandage just drew itself to the animal and bonded. Breanna slowly blinked at Twitch and he responded by slowly blinking back.

"That should do," Brea stated. "He seems settled now." Amber and Kayla just stood there a bit stunned. Twitch and Rocket convalesced for two weeks.

Nine

"The dogmas of the quiet past are inadequate to the stormy present...fellow citizens, we cannot escape history...The fiery trial through which we pass will light us down, in honor or dishonor, to the latest generation. We say we are for the Union. The world will not forget that we say this. We know how to save the Union...In giving freedom to the slave; we ensure freedom to the free—honorable alike in what we give, and what we preserve. We shall nobly save, or meanly lose, the last, best hope of Earth."
Abraham Lincoln

The day was new and was slightly different to the Troyon. The Camps' Overlords stood outside, discussing a confident feeling, a low frequency tone meant to lull the Troyon in a false assurance. Recently the girls did not look up at them adoringly anymore, which made them wonder what could be awry, so this masking tone was used to thwart any discovery. It was the glory of their life for human females to give themselves, these propagation slaves, to essentially die to allow Troyons to propagate. This Troyon confabulation had to be erased. They were told how governments would just abort millions of them until they arrived to save them by subjugating them, and then decimate the remainder of human population, but the truth of self-esteem and human love the spiders brought to the girls' camps on the backs of crows and monk parrots. Three bold figures approached from the east, their featureless silhouettes shadows in the bright morning Sun; this quickly caught the attention of the Overlords.

"Oh make haste and sound the alarm!" The Overlord said sarcastically, the other two acting as if to hide obvious smirks, laughing and gleaning each other on.

"I'm going to keep them alive long enough so they can watch me eat their balls and fuck their woman," the second Overlord said in despicable contempt.

"I'll gut him and make him suck his own shit from his intestine as I disembowel him and watch the life leave his face," the third spoke with a zealous passion, watching the three get even closer.

"It looks as though they're armed with swords," the first Overlord again spoke in utter disbelief. "This is going be fun!" The second Overlord felt a sudden uneasiness, so he grabbed for his side arm. His sense was correct, but too late, Sam and his brothers with their plasmatic enhancements brought them down with lightning speed. Before their next thought Sam struck two and swinging across cutting off his head and one shoulder the body already being turned to plasma and webbing out to all the spiders inside the compound. Their backs arched as the Troyon turned plasma spun from their outstretched swords feeding the foundation of the newly installed spiders taught to the enslaved girls, freeing their minds, feeding their bodies and teaching the truth. Even the youngest was an old soul now, with the knowledge of the network. Troyons began melting everywhere. The plasma streamed on to another, destroying them. The door barely opened as a wisp of a girl slid inside, closed the door and stood silently. The Lord Troy sat there. The Lord Troy was finishing up his morning reports to the High Command—writing well of himself on how many propagation slaves he has sent back to the home world and how many unruly girls had been tamed, and the birthing that had taken place on the planet.

"Come," he said, palm up flexing his four fingers toward himself, "my little pet Goldie." The Lord Troy coaxed her to him with his hand gesture.

"May I speak?" she asked tentatively.

"You are speaking already, you might as well finish," Lord Troy quibbled.

"I need to look you in the eye when I speak to you," Goldie said confidently and affirmatively. She remembered that day all those noisy monk parrots clowning around in the trees, their antics making her giggle. Goldie knew they were helping.

"My little fish shows a bit of strength. That can be a good thing. You know how special you are to me." Lord Troy gave her a name, not just a number like all the other girls. Goldie walked up to him and he scooped her up and placed her on his lap. "You have my full attention little one," Lord Troy said as he opened his eyes wide, staring at Goldie. Her head tilted away, she seemed a little frightened. "Come now, you wanted to look in my eyes," he said, pulling her gaze his way by her chin as her head turned and their eyes met. She thought he knew of the charade. He saw a deep pain in her, and then her spiders jumped right into his eyes. Only a very small amount of plasma began to burn them. He closed them and the burning grew more intense. Lord Troy began flailing. "What have you done?" He grabbed Goldie who was frozen in fear and had fallen to the floor and he picked her up. He flung the child full force toward the wall. Just then the door blew open. Two streams of plasma charged in, one catching Goldie, absorbing the energy and gently placing her down, the other pounded into Lord Troy's head, melting him into a puddle of plasma that was redirected back into the stream, connecting and dissolving more Troyon. Goldie sat on the floor. She was now out of bondage, free—'yet what exactly does that mean?' she thought. Her two spiders, both a little larger from the plasma surge, spun down to her from the ceiling, nestling again in back of her ears into her head. Goldie walked outside. The overlords were in pandemonium, dying in puddles of plasma being streamed away. An older girl walked past.

"Here put this on," the girl said with an ear to ear smile, handing a Life Suit to Goldie who stripped and put the suit on. It conformed to her and looked like a short and T-shirt set. Goldie's fears were being soothed by the communication of Sextant Lori.

"Today we, all of human kind, are free from the bonds of slavery. That void you feel in your existence will soon be filled with the reunion of the union of man and woman. Free life has been returned. So choose your name and you are all pledges to The Sorority of the Ninth Fold, we are all sisters now, and all men are our treasured brothers and will all be looking out for what's best for each other." Lori's voice was soft yet steady and strong, reassuring and resonating. Goldie didn't know what to think. She knew the spiders helped her see the truth and pierce the shroud of dark lies of the Troyon overlords. A crow flew to and landed in front of Goldie. "Edgar!" she said enthusiastically. Placing her arm up the bird flew and perched itself on her forearm. It blinked to her a few times, and then in a raspy strained voice it spoke.

"Goldie." Edgar was there that day too when the monk parrots delivered the spider egg cases. Edgar spoke a few words to her then also. Goldie grinned ear to ear; a Panglossian air filled her and was sent throughout the network, and all reveled in its breath. It was because of Scarlet's great love for the children that she used her familiar to infiltrate the camp. Scarlet would soon be there, but she had other battles to fight first. Edgar ruffled his feathers and shook his head vigorously.

"Aw be back," Edgar's voice crackled as his glossy black wings took to flight. Goldie felt special.

A communication came through. The Uncles were in pursuit of a Troyon ship that was attempting to leave the Earth. Communication had been cut for them but in free space they would get a signal out by one of their booster beacons. The Uncles were in the double snake head fighters. In atmosphere it was a straight cylindrical vehicle, but in space it bowed the internal of the bend that gridded out a power matrix supercharged by plasma-focusing midway from both tips streaming outward in an extremely powerful beam. These are the snake fighters the two Uncles had developed. Now they had to head to the stars to assist the military and give them the plasma they needed to achieve victory, but one of the Troyon ships held over a hundred girls on their way to Troy. They had departed a little early. Because of the attack they would not be allowed to leave the Earth's atmosphere, and send a message to the Troyon home world.

"A situation exists. Precious cargo has a jeopardy fault, must intercept. Tango foxtrot Vega on vector 170 I have an immediate intercept with retrieval before an imminent destruction." Comet the lead comet class fairy put out the call asking for help, needing her sisters to step forward. Rocket flew hard and fast. She would burn through the cargo hold and solder the metal back in place as she entered so the ship would be unaware of her. Rocky burned through and reestablished hull integrity as she entered. She was not ready for what she was about to witness. A hundred and five girls, old enough to be surrogate mothers, but one side of their scalps and many ears were hacked off: the Troyons' solution to rid the girls of their spiders.

Blood spattered the room, a voice speaking calm and reassuring. She was kneeling there beside a girl, her head against the floor. She was holding a compress. "Thirty-three, hold this tight against your wound to stop the bleeding. I check on you soon,"

Number one said. Rocket hovered over to her. When the girl saw Rocket she exclaimed, "Number one here, I got the memory on you Rocket, one through one o' five has different levels of injury, but we'll be ok. What's the plan?" Number one's bandages were already saturated with blood. The Troyon's could not take the memories the spiders already had given them.

"Going to the bridge and wipe them out," Rocket said. A festering hatred exuded from Rocket, a vengeance Troyon retribution. "Get your best five together. I will need help once I have bridge secure," she said. "May I?" Rocket showed Number One a small spider in her hand; she motioned to her permission to put it against her other ear.

Number one looked a bit hesitant but she brushed her hair around her ear to expose her ear as a sign of acceptance.

"Rocket, they number at least thirty strong, be careful."

"Not to worry, I will call you in short order. I will need help ok?" Rocket said, the broken hope in the room giving her a resolute attitude and a seething anger. She grabbed her metal calf guard from her leg it was already hot and heated more in her hand. Rocket looked straight up. Her acceleration was instantaneous, so fast she melted right through the floor. Plasma charged metal spun throughout, finding their marks and liquefying the Troyons. Rocket pushed at the doorway buttons to open a passage to the rest of the ship, riding the flight ball and keeping the ship steady as the spiders figured the control panel. The spiders took in the Troyon ship flight console with the plasma. Several girls came rushing up from the ship. The super charged plasma covering the bridge was a fertile ground for the multiplication of the spiders. A pair of Nano mites hitching a ride with Rocket also replicated geometrically and attached themselves to a number of girls and began mending them. The Nano mites' sympathetic demeanor gave them confidence to accept the new spiders.

"Ladies a little help here!" Rocket asked as the ship rocked in turbulent skies. The spiders directed Number One to the appropriate areas to pilot the flagship. The Uncles were waved off, as the ship turned back to Earth. The fairy Tori arrived at the ship once it landed, first bringing a re-enforcement of spiders and gave comfort to the wounded girls by connecting them to the network. The fairy Tori is an empath who has no speech. Tori was created using Pale Skin's' DNA. Crystal milky hair color and skin the color of cumulus clouds, the body subtle and fine, crystal blue eyes that can deepen to an amethyst purple.

Shades of lotus flower pink colors her lips, labia, and areolas and those blushing ears. Tori used the sensitive ear flesh as an interface to the distressed. As she embraces them she lays her head on them and her ears form a connection. The Nano mites did well healing; Tori would heal the soul. Tori was a fire fairy under Cassiopeia the Queen of Pentacles. Her dress was a sheer Earthen brown flowing, her sheer wispy wings that lay against her as fine silk, but like a filament burn with white fire that allows her flight. Tori's lethalness was challenged by a team of Troyons trying to jump the downed ships. They were met with such ferocity, fire from plasma charged fire wings the produced plasma grapeshot that torched the Troyon like flash paper it even consumed a third of its plasma produced from the immediate over kill charge.

Night was falling quickly, but it was a bright night. Lori would speak in the morning, then survey the area and try to find some semblance of order. Wren went into a chemical sleep, her body so depleted from controlling the Mantiz. Lori thought to sleep too but she...could not, nor did she want to. She flew to the nearest internment camp where inside she saw what she thought was wonderful. The free ones were stripping what they needed from camps. They just wanted to leave, they didn't want to stay in that horrid den of nightmares a single minute longer than necessary.

"Sextant Lori!" they said, greeting in wonder of why she was there. "We need to move out of here," Number Nineteen stated.

"Understood." Lori took one look at her. "Kim," Lori said, the girl's face evoking a buried memory of a friend.

"Kim, you named me!" she said flabbergasted.

"Kim, short for Kimberly, you just look so much like a Kim," Lori stated. "The fireflies will light a path to past that ridge ahead." Lori gestured. "Just follow nature's ques. Ask the spiders any questions when they come back online. For now trust nature; I saw a rally point not far from here."

"I love the name Kimberly, thank you," Kim said, every minute passing, feeling her freedom grow.

"Not to worry. I have a few ideas. First, before you leave take a part of the camp that symbolizes that part you wish most to forget and throw these things in a pile to burn them before you leave. I will fly ahead and recon for our destination." Lori took her hands and placed them confidently on Kim's shoulders. "I will be back after the speech, ok?" A young girl ran out from what seemed like nowhere, amidst the gathering throng.

"Sextant Lori, can you name me? Please!" she begged. "I am Number Seventy-seven."

Lori picked her up in a whisk of motion and said, "You are Clot Hilda, and I will call you Chloe for short." Emotionally tired and scared she showed no fear, but learning the truth of her slavery she did acquire blood lust. Lori embraced the child whole heartedly. Lori took off, surveying what was below her. Lori's head swirled as she thought of what to say and what to do. There was so much gabber on the old networks, people looking for people, information racing back and forth. The spider network then announced it would only have priority messaging until it could revamp certain areas. The Raven was being called for a refit. Wren in her mobile nexus was already being transported for revamping.

"Negative on the refit central. We have to organize for a counter-offensive. I lost communication with Wren central I need access." Lori spoke over the old radio system.

"Raven, please follow uploaded co-ordinates so we can ready your ship for a counter-offensive," the masculine voice said over the radio.

"Now that's what I'm talking about, somebody talking my language," Lori blurted out over the radio. "Swinging your way now central."

Lori hovered over the hanger. Several ships were stationary about the tarmac. She saw movement in the open doorway of the hanger. Three large spiders almost ten feet in circumference were working on a jump ship in the breezeway. Lori landed. As she walked closer to the hanger she saw a stalwart man with a pair of laptops hooked up directly into his forearms. He was controlling the work with the spiders. Not far from the door a few boys looked like they were cooking something on the fire. Lori smelled it, it smelled strange. The beefy guy hooked up to the lap tops seemed a million miles away, not even noticing her. As she walked up to him she put her hand out for acknowledgement.

"Sextant Lori," he said, firmly grabbing her hand. The leads felt onerous. "Sorry they are so heavy but, very busy so I will be as brief as I can." Lori just stared at his cannon ball shoulders and thick neck as he spoke. "Wren is down with a total overhaul, the Uncles have reported a free and clear run and they will rendezvous with the military to give them plasma. Your ship is down because the dark energy flow is overloaded and needs more pathway so, if a counter-offensive comes in we will just have to act out of sojourn again, but right now we need this time."

"One battle and you can't even give me a time when we will be up again," Lori said, her stomach aching from the smell of the cooking. She lashed out.

"Listen," he said, turning her way. "We have a lifetime of wounds to lick, not just one battle's worth. You're hungry, eat something. I hear your stomach growling from here. If you need a transport take my jump ship. Let me get Kaiser to drop my tool container and you can have the ship." He yelled to the boys at the fire-cooking. "Kaiser, dump my container."

Lori felt her folly.

"So sorry, and your name is?" Lori asked as she extended her hand again.

He disconnected the interface and took her hand. "Colin," he said smiling ear to ear. The one larger boy by the fire quickly instructed the younger on the stirring of the stew as he began walking off.

"Do you have a Passenger Container? I have a lot of people in the morning to move," Lori asked.

"Kaiser!" Colin yelled. "Set it up with the luxury coach." Colin motioned to a set of chairs. "It'll be a bit, why don't we both sit down and take a break have a bite and a drink, okay?" he said motioning again to the chairs. Colin wouldn't be hard to talk to, his shoulders were so wide and chiseled. The small boy seemed to walk up from nowhere and placed a bowl of stew and a glass of water in front of her on the table littered with ship components.

"Some," he simply said and looked directly at her.

"Some?" he said quickly, getting no immediate response.

"Yes, Brett, thank you. Can I please have some too, Brett?"

"Yes please I get some." Brett said. He walked back by the fire.

"From dirt baby to sojourn they have a bit of a hard time with social graces, just a learning process." Colin's smile seemed to light Lori's smile as she beamed ear to ear. Once Lori put spoon to mouth the stew vanished. Lori remembered her manners a little late. Lori began yawning, taking in oxygen. She drank her water. Static crackled on the hand held.

"Colin, a bit longer on that ship, needs to transfer hitching device, about twenty minutes," Kaiser informed.

"Ok buddy see you in twenty. We'll save you some stew," Colin responded. "Hey Lori." He was cut off by her rolling yawns.

"What did you put in this stew?" Lori asked.

"Not used to digestion, like eating a turkey dinner huh?" Colin jested. "Rest your eyelids. Going to take a bit of time switching hitches, Kaiser's handling it."

"I can't remember the last time I slept unafraid outside my sojourn," Lori mumbled as she slid into a light sleep. Fantasy crafted her dreams as she was overcome by fatigue. Lori saw herself in a farmhouse kitchen gazing out the window at a slow rolling landscape.

"Like this mom?" Lori turned her young daughter standing on a chair pouring batter into the cupcake pan. Taken by surprise in a dream, Lori skipped a beat before she swooped in to help guide the bowl's batter to the next cupcake cell. "When these cupcakes are done I'm going to bring some to Dad in his workshop." She spoke with the pride of a child doing something for Daddy. "I will even bring Stewie one chooga cake." Lori turned from putting the muffins in the oven and hugged the child.

"Oh! Honey I love you!" Then she was gone, the weather outside looked like an F-5 was ready to drop. Lori ran toward the barn where the workshop would be. Opening the door she saw standing alone was her ship Silver Raven, it seemed to exude energy. Lori quickly boarded her ship and shot straight up. In dream time she was already on a low orbit just before space. She looked at the vastness of space and looked down to the welcoming blue Earth. Looking down at the blue and white of Mother Earth it reminded her of the sky blue and cloud white statues of that Mother Mary that was a mainstay in churches and court yards, and then as she looked into space she pressed her hand against the cockpit sapphire glass. She felt as if she was touching her Father's face for the first time, but that didn't last long. The Raven began to fall from the sky faster and faster toward the Earth, then as it hit, Lori woke stumbling out of her chair and falling on the floor.

"You okay there Sextant?" Colin's question answered a lot. She awoke not knowing when or where she was, but his voice and her question put things in perspective.

"How long have I been asleep?" Lori asked, not moving.

"Seventeen minutes, not long at all," Colin replied.

"I noticed on the way in certain things don't look all beat up and dilapidated, would you know anything about this?" Lori queried.

"Yes I would, seems that the spider's kept an illusion of disrepair as it rehabbed the places it felt we would need. Fact is I worked on a lot of machines. That's where I got hooked up with

95

my two spider drones," Colin said as he showed the tattoos on his arms that masked the integrated hook ups that plugged into the drone's control interface. Energy grid in the ethereal supply energy. "Thing I witnessed is that plasma has flooded through the entire system and as its energy is transformed and directed by the user's emotions and thought, it is setting up a beneficial matrix to our survival. My fervent hope is that this leads to a metamorphosis of Earth born humans to enhance our species that allows us to adapt to our upcoming tribulations. Human-kind is evolving Sextant Lori."

"Too much of a flood of stuff right now, need time to digest it all," Lori said, slowly getting up. "Well thanks for the loaner ship, I will take care of her and I know I will be seeing you again. Where's that ship at anyway?"

"Just follow the fireflies, they will lead you there." Colin stood up, plugged in and began going over the ship with his self-controlled Mantiz. Lorrie slowly followed the fireflies. The small boy ran up to her and handed her a skewer of cooked squirrel meat, to go.

"Free now!" he said and just smiled before he ran away.

Ten

➤ SELF WORTH ◄

The most beautiful people we have known are those who have known defeat, known suffering, known struggle, known loss, and have found their way out of the depths. These persons have an appreciation, a sensitivity and and an understanding of life that fills them with compassions, gentleness, and a deep loving concern. Beautiful people do not just happen. Elizabeth Kubler-Ross

Lori flew, surveying the area. She had a face to face meeting with Wren later that day. The spiders were slow to restart and reintegrate. They had a lot of upgrading and sweeping. So the system was powered down and old kinds of communication were used until the Mantiz system can be fully upgraded.

Flexing streams of fairy light attracted Lori to a remote wooded area. A natural gazebo of cathedral sized trees was lit by a fire burning in the center. The two griffins were engaged in conversation. The fairies disappeared into the darkness of the surrounding woods.

"Did you see that one Troyon thinking he was going to take

me, that didn't last?" Hermes said, Hector ladling another scoop of plasma into his cup, an ear to ear smile on both.

"Yep, drinking him down right now," Hector raved as Hermes' maniacal laugh reverberated through the forest, haunting it with its echo.

"Two incredible soldiers," Breanne said. Lori quickly turned toward her. The three witches were standing there. "They are a bit boastful although right now I see no challenges to their celebration."

"I thank you my sister for fighting so fieacely so that the three of us could be together again," Scarlet spoke. "We must ask you to complete another task." Naomi walked up close, Lori looking soul to soul in each of her eyes. Naomi reached for her shoulders and her hands slid down her arms to hold her hands and she spoke.

"Those who survived refer to you as 'Sextant' because they look for you to guide them in lost times. We believe now that we need a Sexton. The dark times are past but we must still fight. This point in time must have closure." Scarlet and Brea drew closer as Brea went on to explain. "The remains of the fallen will be mourned by all. Everyone will put their prayer and testimonials in a small ball of plasma. They will be collected and placed among the corpses. We shall have a day of mourning and remembering as the plasma directs the emotions. My bodyguards shall ignite the plasma and the dead will be cremated." It wasn't that Lori didn't speak; she couldn't speak. She simply nodded her head several times, tears streaming down her face, and walked back to her ship. This was the first time she could remember that she was able to cry.

After a span of time Lori was composed enough to get back up in the air. That was when another concentration of lights caught her attention. She landed close to a large farmhouse all lit up with a lot of people moving around and carrying meager belongings. Lori walked into the farmhouse. She was overwhelmed by aromas of cooking food. She followed her nose to the kitchen. Several girls were chopping vegetables on the center table and there standing by the stove was Danny instructing the cooking of his special stew.

A raucous group of young men were engaged in horse play. Clasping and legs bending, trying to get one up on each other as they flexed against the railing to their maximum load as they finished down the stairs. A mass of manly flesh was tumbling down to the main level. Lori quickly moved out of the way at the foot of the stairs. One young man peeled from the group and by the time he regained his stance he had Lori on the floor an arm's length away. Lori just looked into his eyes. As he stopped sweat jarred loose from his body, it had an arousing smell. 'This is the closest I have been to a man who is not my uncle,' Lori thought. She then flashed a whimsical smile. ITS charm froze Sam for an instant. She then quickly rolled the both of them so she was on top. By the time Sam realized the change Lori was on her feet helping Sam up one armed. Lori stood there starring at his chest and shoulders.

"You seem a worthy opponent. We should wrestle sometime," Lori awkwardly offered, not really thinking that as she checked out his physique.

"Wrestling is the farthest thing from my mind," Sam spoke with a devilish grin.

Danny' eyes never left the pot he stirred but he proclaimed, "Sam, boys, settle down, we have company." introducing Sextant Lori, the boys were taken aback, not really knowing how to act. They mulled around awkwardly. Sam turned beet red in embarrassment for his forward comment. Lori looked them up and down a bit confounded on her role in this, but she did have an attraction to Sam. She blocked that emotion from hitting the network.

"Would just like to say, we received all the Intel from your frontal assault on the holding camp. Fearless work, so in recognition of valiant behavior as a civilian, all citizens in that group will now be referred to as the Beamer Brigade. This is the most prestigious name for a civilian brigade. I need help with something now. I will begin to ferry girls from the camps. We need them blended in and schooling in mores and values. I appreciate your cooperation in stepping forward."

"Look like I'm going to need a bigger pot," Danny simply said, looking down at his stew pot.

Sam finally found his tongue. "I am very sorry Sextant Lori."

Lori felt his sweat mingling with hers. "This is a time for celebration, not of regrets Sam." Lori put her hand on his shoulder. Her eyes began to probe his gaze, but she quickly broke away as that sensual heat began to rise in her.

"I must go now. Be back soon with your refugees." Lori sashayed to the ship as she wanted Sam to remember her departure, and Lori felt his gaze, unblinking.

Eleven

➤ THE CAMPFIRE STORY ⬅
OF THE ICE QUEEN

I urge you to beware the temptation of pride—the temptation of blithely declaring yourself above all and label both sides equally at fault, to ignore the facts of history and the aggressive impulses of an evil empire and thereby remove yourself from the struggle between right and wrong and good and evil. Ronald Reagan

"This is the story of the Ice Queen, she was also known as 'The Governess of the North'," Danny said as the campfire embers crackled.

"Oh brother!" Jake reeled. "Not again, you have told this tale like so many times." The children would prod his prose by occasionally slipping in a question, probing his perceptions of these tales. Danny loved it so! Yet, for the past five years he only had his crew to tell them to. Starting tonight the new children that comprise part of his audience were born by machine in the Troyon propagation prisons. The grown dirt babies knew the stories, but revisited with Danny and their new found sisters and brothers. The campfire stories and sneaking out of the sojourn were all part of that rebellious hope of being open in this world; those actions fostered that hope including the spider stealth rehabbing that took place.

"Oh now you shush boy, been some time since I put on my vapors." Danny would act out his persona of a storyteller with a boastful swagger. They all knew it was time to pay attention because these tall tales all had a ring of truth to them.

"She was prone and riding fast flat on the deck of an Ice Kayak." The Kayak used a sail to harness the wind. Its bottom had six skis. The rider uses their legs and hips to steer the skis and hand and arms to run the sail.

"Northern winds blew: Northern lights grew." Danny passed his open hand in an arc, looking into the night sky; it was as if he was opening a window to an alternate time, his voice becoming serious. "The Queen was running her rig full out when the spider alert pulsed behind her ear." Looking for her or just passing through, the Troyons were out. Her mission was just too important for discovery. So she zipped up her life suit and jumped out into a snow drift sending the Kayak crashing in the Arctic expanse." Danny reached around to grasp a pouch of Red Man chewing tobacco, the pouch sticking mostly out of his back pocket.

"Now M&M a Sorority Sister to the Ice Queen was trying to get a spider corridor (sojourn) to hide her. Pale Skin was another one of the monikers the Ice Queen held; it was her Sorority Sister name. These women had a lot of (also known as) akas to have enough disinformation to do your best to confuse the enemy. She invited her friend Scarlet into the Sorority of the Ninth Fold. Scarlet was a witch."

"Who is M&M Danny?" the six-year-old Sandy playfully blurted out, retreating into her cupped hands, Sandy wanting to provoke an entire warm spring night of stories. Those nights she listened as she hid in the Earth as a dirt baby, today in the open air was a celebration.

"Who's M&M? Who's M&M?" Danny repeated the question unbelievingly, aghast. "Well some time ago the Ice Queen, MKH, and M&M founded the Sorority of the Ninth Fold. These women were the founding daughters. Upon founding this Sorority they did so with a mystic Sorority of time traveling witches. This cell of three joined with the three witches Scarlet (Sarah), Breanna (Breezy), and Naomi (Nina). Their father Joshua brought them to the past to hide them; problem was he was killed not long after they arrived. This witch's brew of three were pursued so aggressively they used their guile to be innocuous, but were still found.

MKH was just known by her initials. Her aka's were extensive. She had a score to settle with the Troyon. Troyon's never figured how she eluded them. Her folly put them at great unease; she simply killed them. She just woke one day and realized everyone she knew was gone. MKH was a furiously beautiful round shouldered woman, sturdy with thick, beautiful brown hair. The speculation is"—Danny leaned over to a small boy sitting next to him and winked—"that she killed a cavalcade of Troyon and they never really figured out how it happened. She would lure the Troyon to her and just before he mounted her she rolled her head to the side, exposing a vacuumed plunger that would suck their lungs right out of their chests, then she simply disappeared." Danny leaned forward and spat on the fire, pulled back as the fire sizzled, leaned in again and, squinting one eye and slowly shaking his finger in front of his own face, made a point.

"M&M was a piece of work. Pound for pound she made a plutonium bomb look weak. She was petite," Danny overtly looked around comically, peering to the edge of the campfire light, concerned somehow there would be someone at the edge of the light trying to hear his words, so he lowered his voice. Danny's dramatic motions and gestures as he spoke gave the stories a personality. "M&M was of Asian descent born in America. She had stealth implants and an old Victorian treasure. M&M and her crew were responsible for the sojourn deliveries. She was captured they say, I say she allowed them to take her.

Well as the Troyon was raping her she had an old Victorian anti-rape device in her vaginal cavity. Vicki she called it, seems as though they could not extend their shields and be protected and procreate at the same time." Danny made a crazy chopping motion and then stayed perfectly still for a few seconds.

"Augh." When he tried to yell, his voice was breathless; such a muted whisper of a sound never passed his lips. "The Troyons held their voided groins as M&M walked out-unfettered." Laughs and giggles blurted out as Danny's dramatic antics entertained.

"I don't believe that story Danny," Jake questioned as the troop laughs quieted. "These stories are just disinformation, you said so yourself."

"Well now I might have a bit of evidence for y'all now," Danny said as he reached for his staff. A rawhide sack hung just below the top. He untied it and placed the open bag on the ground, exposing an old grey lump of dried flesh. Danny's eyes found Lori's eyes as they made contact. Danny asked her, "Drop a bit of that plasma on that lump of flesh for me would you Sextant Lorikeet?"

Lori was a bit taken aback; she thought no one knew she was named after a Lorikeet. Danny was deep in human penetralia, so trusted as to have such an unfettered filter, Lori thought. Lori walked over to the grey lump pulling her sword out and willed a drop of plasma to run off her sword onto the old grey flesh. It sizzled loudly taking everyone a bit by surprise. Danny saw their hanging jaws as all eyes focused on him.

"Huh? M&M, she's the one of the ones responsible for the distribtion of the sojourns. I was a big supplier for her, got that knowledge out to a lot of the people so they could hide. M&M told me about the Ice Queen. Fact is that's why Pale Skin's alert sounded; M&M was trying to deliver her sojourn. The Troyon was on both their tails!"

"Where did you know M&M from Danny?" Lori asked trying to access an updated story. "How did you know M&M?"

"She was my wife," Danny said, everyone silent and still, in shock, except Jake. Jake slipped around on the ground with his knife. He soaked up half the plasma, his blade drinking like a thirsty rag. He looked up to see Danny's acknowledging wink. Danny's voice broke the record skipping silence. "White on white glare, the snow lightning energy shocked the atmosphere in a milky white glow. Snow blew straight across in fifty mile an hour winds. Drifts mounted on tails of powerful snow devils, howling gale reminds me of those breath stealing winds."

"Pale Skin spent a day in the drift until the weather and the Troyon threat passed. The late winter storm covered all their traces. Pale Skin dusted off; fluffy snow puffed as dry snow fell. Her life suit flexed and reconfigured itself with her mission on hand, alternate transportation. It covered her, completely streamlining her as Pale Skin took to the ice, skating hard, body pulsing in an enhanced euphoria.

Cold steel pounding on unyielding ice, the prototype body augmentations changed her physical appearance; Pale Skin never returned to her normal look, but this did not occur with anyone else. Pale Skin's epidermis turned a glowing paper white. The spider played a Jethro Tull song, 'Skating Away.' The spider let her know her implants were online and she should initiate the final enhancement phase. Pale Skin built speed quickly; she pressed against the infusion bags against her hips, which released the Nanos in their final stage of Pale Skin's evolution: her lips, aureoles and labia were light pink that relished pink of water lilies and jasmine centers, each matching the highlights in her ears' ridges, making them a highly efficient sensory interface. The Nano mites immediately began to reproduce and repair or reinforce Pale Skin's ever pushed body. She felt better by the minute, her implants funtioning more smooth and seamless." Danny's eyes looked left as he recalled, "Her platinum hair washed out in her alabaster skin, her perfectly shaped features lost in an enigma of white. Shadowless light hiding the Ice Queen's symmetrical features, she was just exquisite," Danny explained.

Danny would also tell about how the Governess of the North early on in her quest would dig into the icy water for the salmon she jubilantly ate raw, her fingers and knuckles white with cold. The children around Danny asked questions. Danny's eyes pulled back deep in his own soul as he spoke. "The Ice Queen was the quintessential Patriot, the fifth element of spirit, the essence of mankind. That crazy bastard Pete collected DNA off of her to make some kind of fairy from her DNA, a way to preserve her exceptionality.

The fairy Tori become a splendiferous embodiment of Earth fire spirit. Pale Skin began flowing quicker and quicker across the ice. The warmth she produced was beneficial as her life suit exported the energy it produced to her suit's systems. She felt a tapping behind her ear as the spider communication device clued her in on the location she was looking for. Then she felt it under the blades of her skates, a thin spot that for an instant it was under her skate and she knew she was there. A hollow spot, she glided in a circle coming to rest in front of the ice lenses. The Ice Queen took off her skate and using it as a hammer chipped away at the ice to reveal a tunnel to the submarine Chicago. Warm humid air froze over after she entered the ice tunnel, using her diamond hard nails to slow her down as she descended the icy burrow. She heard the ping of metal under her feet. She cranked the hatch open and the submarine had a breath of life run through it. The sub reacted to her presence. As she closed the hatch and spun the spindle lock more of the systems came online. Pale Skin scanned a map of the ship and headed toward the galley. Sardines and stale crackers never tasted better. Exhaustion laid her right there on the floor in a heavy slumber. Pale Skin's receptors in her ears toned into the hull of the submarine.

She awoke in a dream lying on a wet floor, but it wasn't the floor, it was alive. She was on the back of a whale. Pale Skin heard the moaning and whale's call. Louder and louder it got till the whale noise woke her and she heard them. She felt the hull of the submarine vibrating with their call. Their spirit guided her to initiate the energy exchange grid of the magma containment for the dark matter energy. The initial surge of the energy transfer would be detectable, after that the spiders would have their energy in the dark matter grid and it would not be traceable. The submarine's nuclear reactors would be the pony engine start to energy independence. Cables were connected by the whales and creatures of the sea. Pale Skin knew the energy signature would be picked up and she still had another part of her mission to fulfill and that would be to crack through the ice and fire the specially designed missiles aboard." Danny spit hard into the fire. It burst fire in the air around it like it was kerosene.

"The sub crashed through to the surface after the reactors' heat thinned the ice. Her pursuers had already tracked her as she exited the submarine, hatches blowing to accommodate a missile launched six highly modified trident missiles all were to reach a small payload in a high orbit. Pale Skin's life suit fashioning skates for her as the energy buildt up her accessories gaining more and more power coming from the submarine. The Troyons watched her from a distance aiming their deadly harpoon missiles. Troyons were astounded as a polar bear came out of nowhere and tackled the Ice Queen, diving into the water next to the submarine. The harpoon missiles hit their mark as they exploded into the ice targeting Pale Skin. The Troyons targeted her and not the submarine so enough energy was transferred to start the dark matter reaction. The trident missiles fired up into the atmosphere. The Troyons tracked them but didn't react to them because it was seen as a mere distraction, a Fourth of July firework streaking too high to hurt anything." Danny looked sad. Sandy walked over to Danny and put her arm around him.

"Don't worry Danny she's not dead! The spider sojourn was hiding in the bear's fur like that boy from Kansas. The gateway was mobile because it was stuck in the dog's coat," Sandy stared at him her eyes demanding an answer. "Right Danny?" Danny pulled her close and whispered in her ear.

"I like your tale the best," Danny said as he gave her a squeeze. All those who surrounded the campfire thought back on how this scourge had affected them, how this was not an end but a milestone in the millstone of this arduous journey. Danny's hope was to see his wife: he clung to the slim chance that M&M would be alive, nothing was ever heard about her again. That is all the hope his broken spirit could muster. Danny looked at the faces around the fire, feeling he had to say something. He saw eyes with tears. He figured silence was the best; saying nothing would be saying the most. Sandy glued herself around Dan, her arms around his neck.

"I'm sad, but with everybody out like this I'm not scared anymore," Sandy whispered.

"We sit among the stars unafraid of our openness, yet apprehensive of our future. Gazing into the night sky looking for an answer for what ails us," Dan said.

Lori stepped out of darkness and into the light of the campfire and spoke. "Danny, you know all the stories, can you tell us the story of Dan?" Lori said aching for another piece of knowledge that was filtered from her.

"Okay Lori, how about I tell the story about when our paths crossed?"

Lori's facial expression was a big question mark.

"Yep, your little adopted sister Wren was flying that Heron broomstick south of Milwaukee when our evacuation was overrun by a Troyon squad. I am a good soldier but these guys just don't stay down. All we could do with them back then was to hit them with percussion grenades and air blasters. I got my daughter Kali aboard the evacuation ship. They took off without me because I got hit with some grapeshot in the hip. It took out my hip joint. We were the rest of the military, the last to be retrieved, and a small band of stealth military fighters trying to get to the military space bunker. The military hated leaving the civilians, but with survival of the species on the line, it was thought best to separate. The DOD left everything it had left to civilian's league two Uncles. I would have been dead but seems as though Wren put the broom-stick on auto-pilot that brought you and your dad to Argonne and Wren squirrel chuted down to my position Wren slithered down a tree spiders from all over covered me and encased me into a cocoon of leaves and spiders, she held me close and whispered in my ear. 'Move slowly and be as quiet as you can!'

Wren then shoved a wad of slippery elm where my hip joint used to be, but I was already selectively paralyzed by the spider toxins. I could not scream. The spiders were busy enough stopping me from bleeding to death. Then the line of spider net clicked. I had an executive transport container connected to my jump ship the Pelican. Now I haul around Wren's nexus container, and other types of attachments. The Pelican is a state of the art stealth ship that is used to run supply containers in the back-woods which quickly filled with dirt babies. The spiders then integrated the ship and really kicked up a notch on that invisible invincible state. I got my sojourn that day. Wren and I stayed there two days cloaked. The spiders constructed a malleable hinge with the slippery elm pulp so I would be able to walk as they hastened my healing process. Wren called me out when the forest cleared and we took her returned broom at night to the Pelican. She was well hid. As we entered the spiders interfaced and revamped the Pelican enhancing its functions. I dropped off Wren with her broomstick. I settled down by a farmhouse where the spiders that embraced the stealth abilities of the Pelican and spread into the farm making a reality of serenity with an outward look of deserted dilapidation. This alternate realm enabled man's survival and my house to survive, which grew outward from the farmhouse. Away in my sojourn I longed to one day fill this farm house with laughing bright children." Danny was often out of his sojourn seeking to help those dirt babies and newbies that needed the serenity of his house to make a transition."

"Well then," Lori hesitated then ordered. "Tomorrow I will start sending you children from the camps and I want you to teach them of us."

"Whatever is needed from me Sextant," Danny said, thinking to himself, 'What did I get myself into?'

"Any communications received from the Uncles, Sextant?" Danny queried.

"No," Sextant Lori said quickly. "Which is a good thing, silence speaks."

"Well if I know the military and the Uncles got them that plasma, I really think the something wrong thing is all on those Troyons now," Danny said.

Danny sat by the open fire. He held a cup of hot rabbit mushroom stew. Everyone was tucked away in their beds. He stared at the campfire dancing, and then it seemed as if blades of fire fell from the sky and danced above the blazing fire. The fiery image took a shape of wings and then a flowing flame dress. Danny looked down at his metal cup of stew. 'Boy that's a pretty good batch,' he thought and looked up. The fire fairy danced, slowly revealing her self to him. Her wings became flowing filaments of light, her hair puffy long and platinum blond, her face narrow toward the chin and beautiful, her skin smooth and unblemished, her reddish brown cloths flowing and erotic, her coral pink lips and crystal blue eyes absolutely stunning. Danny heard what seemed like a voice against his own forehead. "I am called Tori."

Danny spoke aloud. "My name is Danny." Tori spun a bit, happy knowing she could communicate with him.

"Don't worry Dan," Tori's thoughts came through. "My sister fairies and I will help you with these girls."

Dan looked down at his empty cup and spoke aloud. "I hope I can remember that recipe and where I picked those mushrooms at!"

Twelve

❧ SADNESS ❧

She is worth more than rubies. Proverbs 31: 10-31

The last throes of that September Sun danced against the glass. Every breath was charged and electric. It was a going away party for the Earth. Our enemies poisoning our planet would be the fuse to initiate the plan, this scorched Earth policy of the Troyon would be their retribution and their demise, but for now the plan was to party, to celebrate the life that this Earth had given to all of its inhabitants. This year's harvest would be the best and this was also a reason for celebration, to utilize their skill set to tame their new home world and reap a great bounty from it. As a slight chill came to the air the domed pool cleared out as people left to get ready. The stage in the outside arena also needed some final prep work as the angst of this world would be thrown to the wind and replaced with a joy filled farewell party. Everyone else was in front of their mirrors primping and preening, readying for an ecstatic night of dance, song, sex, and altered states. Their life suits reading their circumstance, giving each that special dress that accentuated their assets.

Sam and Lori have chemistry between them, but they did their best to conceal their feelings, because Lori, not wanting an enemy to have that Sam card to play on her, and with woman outnumbering men by so many, neither wanted a confining relationship, at least until the move was over. That was all balderdash: the fear was one of loss of another loved one; hide the love, never have to fear the loss. They thought dreamed together. Each really wanting the same thing, that big farm house, enough land to sustain it, to fill that farm with strong children that have been instilled steadfast morals. Have a community of like-minded individuals and spend summer Sundays listening to bands in the park, live free and love hard.

Lori and Sam were going to meet under the dome for some alone time while the party got into gear. Sam set a table for two with a bottle of wine and a spiritual mushroom and cheese pizza. The mushrooms were psilocybin types that were being used to try and gain an insight into the spirit world, and into each other, trying to forge a deeper emotional connection to match the communication of the spider net. Sam floated some candles in the pool. A light misty fog slowly rolling hugged the warm water. Sam was not alone. He looked across the pool. Standing there was Lori. She stood silent taking in her mood setting surprise. Lori's life suit shed itself, dropping to the tiles; Sam admired her soft subtle vulnerable body. As she dove quietly into the pool her undulating body moved seamlessly, a liquefactive motion in all its beckoning beauty. Sam stood there just taking in Lori's being, like watching the mystery of a moonrise.

Lori spanned the pool in one breath. As she broke water Sam's life suit dropped to the floor. The flickering candles, the moonrise, the music from the kickoff of the party created a unique sensual atmosphere. The closer they got to each other the slower they seemed to move, teasing, holding on to the moment of the meeting of the flesh. First a kiss, only lips touching, which drew the two, melding more of their flesh together, then a playful bite to the lower lip. Their hands clasped, from that point their touch and love flowed, knees touching knees, ankles twisting as they gently tossed themselves into the water. Their passion so intense it was a fire unquenchable by the water, but turning that water into a gasoline fire of passionate love.

Lori knew it would be time to leave the Earth soon. She held him close, but suddenly backed off from her intense embrace and looked directly into his eyes, spreading her legs and pulling him toward her. Sam quickly responded, coming forward, holding her lower back entering her. Lori's hands flew back. She began thrashing her hands in the water, a frolicking fish in the sea of life. 'Oh this feels just so right,' she kept thinking. She grabbed Sam's shoulders. The water undulating around them crested as he climaxed. Wrapped together Sam walked out of the pool. Lori dismounted Sam, two heavy bathrobes hung on the rack. Sam was prepared and wrapped one around Lori, then taking his, wrapping himself, and again returning, his arm around Lori.

"Not to make an understatement but, wow! That was extraordinarily stupendous. Do you want this to be exclusive relationship!?" Sam spoke a little incoherently as he walked on his cloud of rapture toward the table.

Lori quickly turned and looked at him, playful anger in her eyes. "Listen mister, we make it to the New World and you better believe this will be an exclusive relationship. I know you have to donate to the bank, but you let me know and I'll help you out." Lori winked as she grabbed the lapel of the robe and drove a kiss on his lips. After a long embrace they backed up and they looked deeply into one another's eyes. A fear of unknowing leached inside as the outward oozing of love squashed all doubt. Sam playfully spun round, grabbing a chair and pulling it out for Lori. She straightened the robe against her hamstrings as she sat smiling and nodding. Sam was pouring wine.

"I have sentinel turret duty at 0500, but we should indulge. Go ahead have some spiritual mushroom pizza. A lot of others are from what I hear," Sam stated as he lit the table candles and sat down.

"I think I will," Lori said, picking up a piece of mushroom pizza and placing it on her plate. "I had Kayla run the numbers on that wormhole for the gamma ray redirection pulsar." Their primary weapon was the opening of a wormhole where pulsar stars were generating gamma rays, and then have the other side open near the Planet Aton and fry it with gamma rays, the wormhole becoming a barrel of a gamma gun. The disturbance around the opening of a wormhole or blackhole is a universal rolodex once locking that in place with a black matter clasp one enters the event horizon and is taken to that destination. Those two missiles Pale Skin fired from the Chicago targeted the opening fringe of a stratospheric wormhole, one going back in time to capture space material and fall back to Earth, the other, a shot into the future leaving a beacon and making a road map of wormhole to open to the gamma pulsar, and void life on Aton. 'All of me' by John Legend was being karaoked on stage at the party.

Sam stood up and swaggered over to Lori. Offering an open hand, he asked.

"May I have this dance my dear?" Sam asked. Lori finished the glass of wine to wash down the pizza, wiped her hands and reached out for Sam's hand; they took a few steps to a nearby patio. They wrapped their arms around each other, the front of the robes open as flesh flirted.

Quietly Lori began talking softly in Sam's ear. "That sex was great, but I want more of it, so you tell me when you're ready for more, okay?" Lori felt his stiffness. "Guess that's just another way of communicating without talking, hmm?" She tongued his ear lobe, as she lightly, teasingly brushed his manhood with the shifting of her hips. Sam softly sang the words to the song 'All of Me' in Lori's ear. "I feel so loved, being serenaded," Lori stated as she pulled Sam in even closer. By the end of the song they were beginning to make love again.

Wren walked into the party. It was outside and the weather couldn't be more perfect. Her life suit's red party dress was slinky and boldly showcased her tattoo interface. The white lights hung all over as decoration became arching rainbows in her mind. She approached a set of friends drinking and enjoying the music. As soon as Wren got close enough Andrea pulled her away from the crowd, wrapped her arm around Wren's head and went forehead to forehead. Her lips then leaned into her ear.

"There are not enough guys here," she stated, her fingers now playing with Wren's nape, foreheads touching, slightly rolling.

"There are more men in space," Wren said loudly.

"That would be great but what about here and now?" Andrea's mouth so close to Wren's ear. "I need some touch." Andrea's light breath of words blew a shiver in Wren that made her body erupt in goose bumps. "Sorry about the chills, seems like you can use a little closeness too."

"I like men." Wren stated.

"Me too sister, but there are not enough men here. That flesh to flesh touch is just so ever soothing." Andrea's spoke the words so seductively. "Hey, if you convince some guy to go with you, tell him he can have two if you're willing to share. Same with me: if I get one and you want to share with me we can have good time." Andrea's fingers lightly caressed Wren's interface tattoos. Wren's eyes almost rolled in back of her head, such a soothing relaxing caress her defenses dropped. It just felt so calming, so right. "We'll catch up later okay," Andrea spoke softly right in her ear. As she pulled away Andrea lightly kissed Wren's cheek and Wren in that moment kissed back as Andrea pulled away and Wren awkwardly kissed her back. It landed right smack on Andrea's lips. Wren took a step forward, trying to follow her; the step woke her from her trance. They stood for a moment, longing eyes flirting. Andrea didn't know why she was so attracted to Wren; maybe Andrea's large heart had what it takes to heal Wren's soul. Not that there was any shortage of pain in the population it just that theirs' fit. All Wren knew is that she made her feel erotic and warm. The Brittany Spears song 'Till the World Ends' brought everyone to their feet, dancing and fist pumping the air. Andrea grabbed Wren's hand and drew her to the dance floor.

Everyone was on the dance floor. It was just a good time; everyone was singing along, dancing. Lori and Sam then walked in as Linkin Park 'Crawling' was being performed. Sam and Lori stood nose to nose on the dance floor singing at each other, the words sticking in Lori's brain, the verse so close to her emotional state, as the song played out and changed to 'People Like Us' by Kelly Clarkson. One by one people started looking up, facial expressions of excitement spread as more eyes focused upward. Lori and Sam looked up and saw Brea, Scarlet and Naomi flying their Blue Heron brooms in a triangle formation, slowly coming down on the dance floor. 'Our witches are here!' That was the repeated phrase traveling through the throng. The three landed as the dance floor cleared a landing zone.

They came around and spoke to a people now and again but everyone knew of them from their dreams. The three were sadly secluded, but in dreams they showed an emotional cosmos of flawless design. Everyone came by, greeting the witches. Brea had a strapless red polka dotted dress, shear long white gloves, her witch's halo all aglow. Scarlet's jaw dropping red dress highlighted her milky white skin. Naomi had on an airy red floral print dress that had a plunging back. Her dragon tattoo as it was called was curled up on her shoulder and scapula. As Lori and Sam made it through to Brea, Sam gave Lori a long hug and lasting kiss. He had to crash a bit to make it to turret duty. A glance around and Hector and Hermes were standing close by in their human veil.

"Now, you ladies have fun and take care of my Lori for me okay?" Sam said to the group, as he looked in Lori's eyes holding her hands. He turned and left. 'Summertime Sadness' sung by Lana Del Rey and all the dresses turned hot red for the song. Naomi and Wren talked to each other about their functioning tattoos. They and everyone there found a comfort in each other they did not have before.

The sound system was set to play music as the party wound down. Small groups socialized and chilled. Andrea approached Wren with a man in tow. "Hey girlfriend, Stevie and I don't have anywhere to go. You got any ideas Wren?" Andrea said, biting her bottom lip and shifting her eyes toward Steve.

"Sure, we can go to my jump house," Wren said. "Bye-bye." Were heard as they waved their farewells.

Andrea swung Wren between them as they walked. Steve reached over for a kiss from Wren. As they kissed Andrea squeezed Steve's butt, and grazed her hand across Wren's bum as she brought her hand back to her. All Andrea wanted was Wren's euphoria so she could get some of Wren's touch. She thought Steve okay, but her healing heart wanted Wren.

The male population as a gender was confused. They deeply loved woman and wanted to propagate and sought to be more protective of its female population. Men were seeking a more common core with their counterparts. The female population, once they saw through the shroud of lies, their biological hardwire took hold. They were guardians of the species, unforgiving and aggressive to their enemies. The dark heart of woman revealed in its turn around, as survival of the species trumped all.

The morning couldn't have been more complicated. It was a minute to five. Andrea was spooning Wren and Steve was nowhere to be seen. They were in Wren's round bed adjacent to her nexus container. The klaxon sounded; yes, it was the end time. Wren put her finger across Andrea's lips so as to shush her as she tried to speak. "All this was really nice and you were just fabulous, but I don't know if I am all this; so how about we survive the next twenty-four hours and see where this goes." Wren replaced her fingers to her lips, kissed them and pressed that kiss against Andrea's lips. "We got to go, I have no time," Wren said as she already had Andrea out the hatch. The Pelican aurora class flying frame was already docked, with her nexus container locked on as she got in her tiger interface and began establishing communications with Lori. Danny immediately took off, heading to Florida to drop off Wren and evacuate as much as he could as fast as he could. He was also to pick up a military co-pilot to help monitor the military that was already in the field. This was a joint operation. Other than remote drills the two factions had never met. Dan thought it might be best not to mention his military past.

Thirteen

⇾ DARK HEARTS ⇽

"We have used the new arm of our minds to survive. Now we will use all three arms to slay our enemies, in cold blood and with dark hearts," Sextant Lori

"**B**roken fence! I repeat we have a broken fence. Grids on nineteen to one twenty-two will initiate sanitation of grids ninety-nine to one fifty in seven minutes. Setting all turrets to auto-sanitation in same seven," Sam spoke. There was Troyon detected. The turret retracted its leg as it settled on the ground as the other sectors remote turrets legs deployed and held them up above the tree line. The klaxons alarm shocked the blurry headed revelers into lock step all going to action stations.

"Retrieve occupant of turret nineteen," the command spider network relayed as the alarm died down. The Rapid Retrieval Response on station was already in action, their life suits converted to combat suits. The dark energy established a direct conduit to the suit. It gave it storage with no mass to be summoned by the wearer upon command. The suit gave you the look of a black silhouette. You become a shadow with an inventory of whatever the mind can conceive. The VTOL Aurora class jump ship with the rapid deployment container was warmed-up and in ready one. Most just slept inside, a few others yards away. The Mini-14s were in the rack with plasma soaked magazines. Several squads rotated this battle station readiness. The door barely closed as the jump ship popped into the air. A fast hard landing and everyone was headed out the door. A secure perimeter was quickly established as the two escorts entered the turret. Full action alarms sounded in the townships. 'Everything just became two weeks early,' Lori thought.

Sextant Lori spider relayed, "Evacuate Sam from turret nineteen. Sanitation begins in five minutes, secure and move. Take him to the rally departure point and go for primary push off."

Wren laid it out in front of Lori and she concurred with the sanitation. Lori pushed the timetable up hard. Lori felt Sam's emotion hit her with a lot of anger through the spider network. "No!" Lori said tersely. "Stay on mission; because it just got real premature, this just became a slugfest. We were supposed to depart before the Troyon got here. I need that push off area in Florida secure as of now." Sam knew immediately she was right: it was time. Troyon would now come to destroy humanity and their planet, by polluting their home with their venomous scorched Earth policy.

The Beamer Brigade was already en route to Florida and communicated to Sam to get a move on it. Their first scan showed several waves of Troyon stealth gliders infiltrating the atmosphere. Wren was notified.

Wren's entire field of work dealt with the advancement of the 'Gladiator class AI mantis.' This highly capable bionic predator had the artificial intelligence to fly at scram jet speeds without dumping in the ocean. Unmanned its speed exceeded twenty Mach. These vessels were hypersonic. It was initially a spider design but, after the freedom fight a more aggressive weapon was needed, so it took on the physical characteristics of a praying mantis. It favored the devil flower mantis, orchid mantis and the fire mantis. These predators were scary as hell. One look as that triangular head with those cold red eyes and horns would make your mind gulp in fear. The Gladiator class was man sized. It was also fully capable as close air support or hand to hand combat. Marauder Class was larger and very capable in air to air assault. Its power pod system can even take it to orbit outside the power net with agitated plasma as fuel. Plasma molded its kill power potential through the AI since no emotions were present. The sojourn key spiders kept their form but were able to quickly transform to the mantis type if a more aggressive stance was needed.

Wren's work in achieving a neurological net, her brain hard-wire was the template of the artificial intelligence used in the network. Wren did give a gift to Sam during the initial jump to the rally point: Wren sent a thousand of what she named a Chippewa Class mantis. They were about the size of Camel Spiders and just as sinister as the Gladiator class. These were also winged. They were used for web security at the rally point and were close rear guard to the Beamer Brigade. Sam fought the notion at first but when Lori described the tactical advantages, the Brigade's entire strength can be used as a forward spear allowing the Chippewa to anchor the rear and guard the flanks.

Lori double timed it across the tarmac. She was to meet up with a military flyer named Kali; two Marauder class fighters mantis would complete their tactical unit. That song 'Crawlin' by Linkin Park stuck in Lori's head. She dissected the lyrics. Lori's insecurities plagued her. She had to buy more time. This counter-offensive was going to be everything the Troyons had. The ground crews were too busy to pay much attention to Lori's unsure steps. Raven was so shiny like a freshly minted proof Peace Dollar. The curls in the wing pits were very avionic. Lori melted into the ship's liquefaction system and took her place under the sapphire canopy. Lori grabbed the joystick. An optic spear connection shot into her hand. The pain faded quickly as the nerves were blocked. A wave from the ground crew and Lori upped the throttle and began a takeoff run. Wren told her that Kali was now in the atmosphere. Before she could think the Silver Raven took to the air and gained altitude quickly. Then it happened: the AI rebooted and put Raven in a flat spin. The Troyon got a piece of virus on the AI program on that didn't get destroyed fast enough so after the virus was killed the system auto-rebooted, but it was a bad time.

Kali was flying fast and low, taking in as much of the land-scape as she could. 'Earth is a gorgeous planet,' she thought. 'How sad this day that the Troyon scorched Earth policy would poison the planet, but what a wonderful mother she has been to her inhabitants and universal adventurer it has birthed-man. A mother so loving she will be shredded and reconfigured to insure its offspring.' The kaleidoscope of land and sea around Kali made her shiver; looking at the beauty of Earth she had no doubt that this awesome Mother Earth was capable of anything. Kali was honored to be fighting side by side with her civilian sisters who together would destroy those who have poisoned their home and killed Mother. Disinformation had set asunder the military and the civilian people and Kali wanted to reinstate her loyalties to the people. The military armed with plasma decimated the Troyon's when they raided their home planet, taking back as many people as they could. The spiders the Uncles brought with them ensured them a sense of belonging and worth they had never had. Truly a hideous Troyon plague they had encountered. Then the Troyons lashed out with their counter-offensive.

"E controls to Kali, come in Talon," Wren transmitted on the spider.

"You have Kali in Talon. Go ahead control," Kali responded.

"I have a situation. You are in range and I need you to do a maximum ascent under Raven. Lori is stuck in a reboot spin. Her avionics cannot reconfigure unless you wash out below her. Her AI picked a bad time to boot out a virus," Wren relayed and

Kali immediately responded. Kali was in a Raptor 32 thunderbolt that had been refitted. The spiders realigned her ship with a dark energy conduit that delivered more thrust, more maneuverability and one heck of a weapons system. Kali came here to be the best and to prove that the military was going to lay it on the line just as hard as the civilians. By the time she saw Raven's blip on screen she was executing a power ascent below her. Kali felt a blackout close. The mantis system took control until Kali recovered. Raven was jolted in the wash and Lori's connection to her hand was streaming AI in and out of her, creating a single entity vessel that was battle fierce.

"Thanks for the wash, Kali. Are you ready to kill some Troyons?" Lori asked.

"I am ready to kill them all Lori, on your wing," Kali replied. Two hypersonic Marauder class mantises joined them. As the other mantises filled the sky the enemy rained down like a violent meteor shower, but the Earth forces engaged just as strikingly. The plasma surge devastated the enemy. The Troyons were not ready for this type of onslaught. The aerial bursts of plasma wiped out entire Troyon air wings.

Wren spun in her control module, suspended on her fiber interface cables, monitoring flight action and directing assets. More assets were now being directed to flight than fight. One Troyon Armada remained; Kali was called to the surface for a mission. Lori and many mantises still fought the Armada but their flagship was very powerful and proficient. They centered on Lori, surmising she was the leader. The battle was in its final stages. The Troyons got through and poison was released on Earth and Lori hoped she had gained the time to allow everyone to evacuate. She knew the remnant of the Armada would center on her. They followed her as the rest of the Earth air wing went back to mop up because the Troyon ground forces took just as much of a shellacking.

Rocket raced into the engagement. Kayla was out front with her mantis crew slaying Troyons. Amber was fighting then flanking. Rocket spun a plasma lasso around several Troyons and quickly tightened, destroying them.

A winded Kayla was on her knees, a Blue Heron broom lying on the ground next to her. Rocket and Amber went over to her. Kayla handed Rocket Pete's reader with the location of the dark anti-matter fuse.

"So, you okay KK?" Rocket asked. Amber came to her side and helped her on her back.

"They can fix anything Rocket," Kayla whispered. "Light them up Rocket, light em up." Rocket took off. Her emotions wanted her to stay and help but she knew she had a job to do. Rocket flew to the first location. She saw the tree at the end of the rocky field and headed there. Inside the hollow yoke was a small sapphire orb containing the filament of dark anti-matter energy. Rocket picked it up and looked closely at it. As she began to fly out of the tree an energy net pulled her down to the ground. In an instant the Troyon's were around her.

"See these creatures do exist, and we just stopped this one." The Troyon boasted. Rocket tried but she could not project any plasma to destroy the Troyon. Then Rocket felt it, through the net, a familiar wind. Before she even thought his name his claw swiped and just annihilated the enemy.

"Hector!" was the name Rocket was about to think.

"Yes," Hector stated, plucking the net up like a piece of lint off Rocket. Rocket in turn gave the best hug she could around his cheek, but only hugged one of his scales. "You got time to make up, little one. I will give you a boost." Rocket was off as Hector threw his friend as hard as he could to give her a boost.

"Taking a shepherd's orbit," Lori relayed.

"Roger shepherd orbit Raven," Wren replied. Lori hung there suspended between Earth and the heavens, one hundred and thirty-five thousand feet up almost in space. Lori was trying to figure out how she was going to be able to survive. Lori felt a kindred swoon toward her ship. It gave her that awareness she was blessed with flight. The only way for her to survive was to have all three survive. It started like an itch that couldn't be scratched the spider behind her ear bit to get her attention. It was Wren she was sending a plan. "Come down bulk first make your trajectory to hit the center top panel that will be the last one closed. At scram jet speed your ship will break apart. A sonic plasma spray will make a shifting plasma mine field to destroy the rest of the Armada. You have available charged metal you can eject, you will blow right through and incinerate the remaining Troyon Armada. Transfer anything you can from your ship into your life suit and available cell space. At that point of plasma transfer engage your turbo then enter your sojourn as a single entity. Safeguarding the AI of your ship, together you may survive the impact. "

Lori was positioning herself for the power dive, waiting for a go light. She would blow the excited plasma through the turbine, which would send her to a hyper scram jet power dive. The remaining mass not used in the offensive would burn off and spray a plasma field, destroying any remaining ships.

Lori felt a stirring chill run through her as the reconfigured core of the ship flooded her being. Only because of the baby who's life she felt start inside her womb did she for the first time fear Wren's last words: "You may together survive the impact." The Nanos worked feverishly adjusting the ship; Lori fired the retro rockets trying to give an impression she was going to shoot for a higher altitude, keeping the Troyons thinking. The Troyon captain of the flagship pursuing her would make a fatal mistake if he tried to dog her, but this Lori was counting on, that his aggressive nature would be his own downfall.

It was time for Lori to show her metal. She was coming into her window. She felt a spider pulse from Wren. "Good journey sister!" Lori knew her hands were full. The fight below finished up missions and mopped up, the poison was dumped in a remote area and it would be a day before it reached them, by then all would be gone. The power grid from the dark energy mantle flooded the atmosphere and Lori's plasma pods. She would fire up and go full reverse, enabling the most massive part of the ship to melt away and producing enough thrust to achieve maximum velocity. The important parts of the ship would cascade down and into Lori, entering the doorway to her sojourn. Some remaining metal of the ship and the AI would be inside her with her unborn child before impact. The problem was she was not sure spiders can completely close the door in time so a metal molded physical door would be made to close the gap, and the crash energy must be transferred back to the power grid or it would burn them to oblivion. To accomplish this Raven would have to make a thermodynamic metamorphosis and become a molten unit dispersing its mass, spinning off into a plasma rain of death for the Troyon pursuers until a concentrate of Lori would be left and the artificial intelligent and digital memory stored in Lori's cells. The metal of the ship was replaceable but its plasma enhanced function and memory had an artificial mind of its own.

Lori pressed her one free hand against the cockpit glass. She looked out into the beauty of space she had so longed to see. She felt as though her hand against the cockpit sapphire glass, as if she was touching the face of the eternal Father. Lori tapped her vision into the spider net to check on things. Sam and Trent found themselves by the barrier islands at the tip of the Florida Peninsula. The Bermuda Triangle would be the epicenter of the vortex. They were to surf the wave (Florida as a cosmic surfboard) from the vortex. They would pick up the Asian hemisphere inhabitants and some of the Japanese islands, to form the vessel Earth. People had been moving to Florida with their Sojourns for a while now. Wren was running air traffic for the military ship's landing. The military people took well to the spiders, but some in space were still apprehensive of them. ('But why?' Lori thought.) Were they more comfortable hanging around in the old closed amusement parks socializing? Lori fired the engines and began her power descent to the rally point. This energy dome was in the process of filling the grid with its energy hull for the voyage to their New World in this Earth vessel joining with its eastern island on the other side of the Earth vortex in the China Sea. The key was to start the full power descent, and blow right by the Troyon flagship.

Lori felt the heat in her palm, as the AI transferred itself. Its AI had been boosted by the plasma. This would be her Phoenix ship. The Silver Raven morphed into a liquid hull as the ship sped up and it took the form so that the flaring ship acted as a single turbo now expelling the scramjet fuel and blowing by the Troyon ship that quickly took pursuit. The molten metal blew off the ship quickly eliminating the Armada arrayed against her.

The energy field was being formed around the rally point. The top of the upper half of the dome top would be the last to fill in and Lori's target. The Silver Raven was a molten speeding vessel burning itself smaller, dissipating at its thirty Mach speed. Any Troyon ship behind it hit the energy field and was obliterated. The ship burned in a fiery magnesium white light burn. As it spread the sky shuttered it white luminous glow as a capsule made it to the ground, in a spectacular fountain of molten metal. It was the MOAF (mother of all Fourth of July fountains).

There hovering quickly down, now tumbling end over end, sounding like a shot pheasant, Rocket followed Lori in. Her energy depleted body pulled in to safety by her spider connection to the AI picking up her signature. Jessica the Lunar fairy came to assist her. She was a fair-sized double moth winged luminescent green lined in glowing purple matching the flowing garments sheer and soft. She touched her shoulder. Coolness spun down around Rocket. Energy emitted from Jessica's hand started rejuvenating Rocket. Jessica's empathy and Rocket's predicament attracted Tori. Tori nuzzled her ears against the tattered wings. Her energy of heart also fed Rocket's recovery. Tori's eyes looked into Jessica's eyes; her soulful expression showed her great sadness of her sister's injuries, yet her pride of her great courage, that look of knowing that she would be well, with their love and care. The two carried Rocket off to a fairy place where she could be tended to.

The Beamer Brigade and a small contingent of military security raced to Lori's crash site. The shell of the capsule was already cool and cracking. There were no open flames or fire so they did not foam or use and dry extinguishers. The energy had been transferred back to the grid. The metal around her just seemed to go up in vapor, leaving her body so still and depleted, yet loaded with two others. Sam just stared at her for a moment then slowly moved down toward her, kneeling now, and then bending, giving her a soft kiss on the cheek.

"Open a path to her to get a medical team in and see what's going on with her," Sam ordered, while he tamped down his emotions. A medical transport came in with Amber inside to hook up and monitor; she fed live feed to Wren to get her take on what had transpired. The Silver Raven expended all of its metal, saving its pilot but at the same time the density reading was showing that the essence of the ship had melded with Lori somehow giving the three a chance of survival. Lori was taken to the medical unit for observation. She weighed at least fifty pounds more but she was same size her density had changed.

Lori's eyelids slowly open the voices of the people in the room a distant garble. Lori began to remember who they were.

The military conference room was having a briefing before the squad was sent to Earth. The Lieutenant General walked down the center of the room. Like their own heritage of Earth they wore life suits. Theirs were more adapted for the rigors of space battle and not the stealth guerilla warfare of its relatives on Earth.

"We have finished debriefing the Uncles and we have built our campaign on the reintegration and the survival of humankind. You will be first contact and liaison a strained relationship between civilians and soldiers." The LG looked around at the squad, his bald head gleaming under the LED lighting. "Your mission will be to halo to Earth in striking distance of a facility known as the Argonne. You will follow their protocol and take on a spider to link you to their people and be on your best behavior."

LG felt their unease, but their choices were only the one. "Without this spider device you will be hunted out and destroyed by the survivors. They are aggressive and very protective and still have a bad taste in their mouth from what they see is the military running away and leaving them all to die." He stopped and turned one way then the other. "We must change that perception. They must be made to understand that that perception is the one that our enemy has put forth, to push forward their agenda. After seven days of going over details and debriefing the Uncles. My advice to you to change this perception is to show them the reality. You are to be the outstanding troops that you are. These are our people; we have given an oath to protect. We will unite to survive the final chapter.

The adaptation of the spider realm and the changing the laws of physics gives them a subculture to endure the occupation. Whether it is crucifixion, the inquisition, the Nazis, Stalin, Mao, Khmer Rouge, Saddam, Syria or the Taliban inflicting deep pain on everyone, it will be no more. No matter when in history or where in the world, rape is rape, murder, murder. As non-humans now the Troyans have learned from past transgression on man and exploited all Earth and its inhabitants. Their belief is that they have sown the seeds of civilizations and it was theirs to be harvested. I am not good at this. I am a soldier, but we must be at our highest regard for mending these bruised perceptions of one another. Alright then, get to your jump ships; we have a war to win."

The squad moved quickly through the field. The baby sat in the middle of the freshly harvested corn field. The child screaming, the squad moved tentatively to investigate and saw spiders crawling in and out of the baby's ear and around her eyes.

I fear the event of death as I fear the memory of birth;
Fear of life; Fear again of a long life
Living in squalor oppressed by a thing,
A nightmare Beast

So I have Life, a life lived for memory
Seasonal splashes of color;
Newly painted trees
Heavy laden fog; blankets
Water like snow-forecasting
Sun's embers push at the soot of night
Crescent moon starts to melt
Growing morning light
Nostrils rasp cool dawn air
Filling hungry lungs
Chest expands
Breathe fresh Earth air
Breathe Life
Fog of Breathe
Exhale
Shutter;
Shiver
Stillness
Breathe

The camouflaged tarp cracked off the tenuous frost. The soldiers came from under stretching and moving for blood circulating warmth. The fog frost covered everything in Jack Frost fuzz. Joanne looked around, her mouth slacked open in awe.

"Is it always so beautiful here?" Joanne asked Kali. Joanne's tall frame cast a steamy fuzzy shadow. Ice fog converted back to fog in the morning Sun, a lone crow cawed to the new morning.

"It's just so pretty and calm here," Joanne said, moaning and stretching like she just got out of bed.

"Yo Jo, no kip till we connect!" Kali chastised, but wondered why. "From what I remember it is beautiful here," Kali stated. Memories of her escape and leaving her father here injured and dying her only defense was her convincing herself. 'Danny was dead.' The spiders would discover their relationship soon after the implant and the DNA analysis became common knowledge.

Joanne fought with a thought: Did I fall asleep, and did I doze? Why didn't I snap out of nodding off? Should I say something?

"Hey, has anybody here had a strange dream, or feels out of phase or sorts?" Joanne spoke, anxious about the feedback. "You should move quickly and take to the trail," she heard clearly in her head. Kali was startled, but then understood that the spiders had already found their targets. They all had spider communication. As they walked the trail, the squad recounted they had the same dream of a baby crying in the field and as they each went to investigate they saw a spider run to the back of the baby's head and tuck itself in. No one remembered falling asleep. Guess that was the spider way of telling them that they were connected.

The squad stayed on the trail, the spiders guiding them. The warming air chiseled the frost away from the trees and let the colors come through.

A short distance down the path stood Hermes. He stood as a shrouded man, cloak as dark as night, the strong smell of Basil permeated him; his cloak shimmered in the ambient light like a raven's plumage. The spiders told the troop he was an official bodyguard sent to accompany them on their first mission.

"Kali; Joanne and I will take your squad on the ground. Here is a Chippewa rear guard. It will show you to a refitted Raptor 32 thunder bolt you did your simulator work on. You will be flying wing with Sextant Lori, then air support for your own team's evacuation. Your bodyguard will lead you." The two were off. Kali was an excellent pilot and had flown ground support for her squad before, but the Raptor 32 thunderbolt was the type of plane her dad had flown. This coincidence spooked her a bit. "Jo!" Hermes continued. Joanne's eyes flared open. "You and your team will sweep in back of me, mop up, repel any flanking action, and aid homesteaders so they can be transported to our rally point." Hermes turned into his warrior self battle axe wielding body shifted soldier as thirty Troyans came to overwhelm them. One swing of his battle axe and they all became a puddle of plasma.

131

"Beware of a second wave on my six," Hermes warned as the team moved.

"We got your back big guy!" Joanne reassured. "Sure glad this guy is on our side." The spider network laughed, hearing humor in her words.

Joanne's Squad tore through in back of Hermes, mopping up a feeble second rush. The sounds of the Troyons' pulsars got their adrenaline flowing. They stopped before a homestead clearing and met stiff resistance.

"Gel them!" was heard all around. The battle was intense yet short lived. The crescendo of arms fire just stopped. They moved to the farmhouse as other fighters rallied there. The team set up for force protection as the emergency jump ships came down and the citizenry were evacuated. Joanne surveyed the area as she walked over to her new CO Hermes. Several of the higher ups were conferring with him. A badly injured soldier was being transferred to a medic jumper. I heard bits of their conversation between the favorable wind and the chatter of the spiders. This fighter was well known and well liked. The upper echelon broke and I saw him, a male human badly burned near lifeless, a once beautiful human desecrated by the ravage of war. Hermes and a woman approached Joanne and the woman spoke.

"My name is Kayla." Kayla spoke stoically. "That's my dad they are taking, he was diverted here off mission because of a distress call. I need someone to finish his mission, are you up to task?" Kayla had a bit of a hollow choke in her throat as emotions festered beneath her war calloused skin. Kayla's arm came up and rested on Joanne's shoulder. The other hand pointed to the tree ridgeline. "I have a four-year-old child that was taken in ceremony. She is now only with spiders; Jo you will go in and retrieve the child and make it to your extraction point. The pattern above you is so full of dog fight, and the area is not secure by any means so you will secure that zone by any means necessary. The spiders and Nanos are already reconfiguring your suit. All your gear will go with your squad. You and your suit will be running on dark matter energy. Think it and it will be supplied to you, and I promise you will be the most badass and fastest thing ever on this planet."

"Will do, can do whatever is asked. Let's do this," Joanne said confidently taking pride in the fact that she was taking the reins for Kayla's father.

"Well!" Kayla said raising a syringe toward Joanne. "I don't have time to do the prep work for a pain block, so sorry but this is going to hurt bad, real bad." Joanne's eyes closed as Kayla gave her the injection in her neck. All Joanne kept hearing was like an echoing, "Real bad, real bad."

Joanne woke up in mid stride. The suit had taken off with her as a passenger. Joanne was firing lighting plasma, which lit the forest, blowing a path through the Troyon squads trying to advance on her. The memory of pain was gone, replaced with 'o yeah girl you real bad' as she tore through to the child's position. The cold rolled steel coiled boots gave her advanced running and jumping power even though it looked like something Willie Coyote thought up. Joanne arrived at the child's location and spiders melted the child right into Joanne's life suit and they were off running.

Joanne would need all energy diverted for a speed slow down before the evacuation point; she hoped Kali would get the last leg of her journey sanitized so she could stop in time.

Kali landed rough, she had to hand sanitize the rear area of her landing zone to cover her escape. Joanne would take the observer seat, a back to back rear facing seat in her ship. Some missions needed gunners or techs, this mission was an evacuation so they traveled light. The on board computer spoke, reviewing the procedure as Kali walked down the emergency stairway that emerged.

"Locate sanitizer storage compartment on the underside of the fuselage. Turn handle counter-clockwise until pressure is released and pull handle out. The door swung open. Stand under opening under marked balance point, pull yellow handle above launcher. Launcher will rest on shoulder. Walk facing area to be sanitized. Lean forward until launcher slides to ground. Pull blue cord until tripod unfolds. Pull launch cylinder up, unfold leg anchors and press red button on lower third of cylinder to blow anchor nails in ground. Unlock launch cylinder, pull trigger assembly, which will activate launch mode and battery will power discharge ignition coil. Aim in sector to be sanitized and fire."

Kali's eye flooded the targeting scope. She set the power to maximum. The spider in her ear told her to be ready, and they were close and closing fast. They were. Her heart pounded as the spider counted down before she appeared over the hedgerow. Once she cleared Kali fired. The rocket rose up to proper altitude and exploded. Kali felt the plasma burst as the shockwave hit her. Blown, faltering, Joanne wrapped her arm around her waist and began pulling her, helping her move faster toward the ship. Kali loudly spoke only one word. "Move!"

Joanne was tall and top heavy. The child was wrapped in her life suit around her torso, Kali tried to hurry her exhausted body. Joanne conduit disconnected from the dark energy as she grabbed the ship's ladder. She appreciated Kali's help as she guided her up the ship's ladder. Giving her a boost, Jo's spider instructed her on the pre-flight buckle in check list as Kali donned her helmet and turned up her idling ship.

Extremely loud turbine vents turned downward to give the ship lift. Checking her stores Kali was down on just about everything, fuel to sidewinders. Soon as she could she ran full throttle out of there. She was gaining altitude. Kali saw two ships coming up and another vectoring in. She set her last M.O.A.B. device as an altitude depth charge exploding the bomb at the altitude of the pursuing ships. The concussion blew the two ships from the sky. The third charged toward her, sending an array of ordinances her way to keep her busy. Kali messaged out: "Visitor Two low on stores requesting a refill and an assist V.T. P.A." Jump ship Pelican seemed to come out of nowhere with missile counter measures. Nexus one also sent a ground based pair of sparrow missles that would find their mark.

"V.T. Deuces come back on concerns," Danny spoke over the radio. Even though the spiders keep the communications open and fast, to Kali a voice on the radio was reassuring. Before hearing any more chit-chat, an answer from Kali's anti-ordinance halos spun from the ship's fuselages. Missiles exploded close to V.T. The rear avionics were Swiss cheesed. Kali's stick got heavy and shaky. "V.T. is declaring an emergency. We have a mayday."

Kali and Jo knew they couldn't eject for a ground pick-up now. It would be suicide. Poisons were probably already released on the surface and they had a new place to get to. Danny gave it a shot. Kali was to maneuver to the rear cargo hold. Danny would open the door and Kali would have a spider trail some plasma six feet back from the cockpit, then Kali would ignite the plasma. The aggravated plasma would burn and push the cockpit into the open cargo bay.

A spider laid a line of plasma around the inside of the fuselage behind the cockpit. Kali set and burned off the fuel, which activated the plasma ring. The plasma burned them clear but the push was a bit off and the tip of the ship came through cockeyed, bouncing about. The fire suppression blew fogging the cargo hold. The ship's front antennae went through the bulkhead and impaled Danny to his chair. Carol rocked in the chair shaken to near unconsciousness. Looking in front of her at the flight console she saw it speckled in red. Turning to Danny to ask what happened she saw the metal poking out of Danny's shoulder pinning him to the chair. A large spider about the size of a fist was already on his shoulder webbing it closed, trying to stop the flow of blood.

Behind the speckles of blood she knew the constant flashing consoles lights were not good, and she was in control so to speak. She would be making the calls, losing telemetry to the cargo hold. Carol pulled up on a heavy stick. She wanted as much altitude as she would be able to get. The strike alert chirped incisively in her head, a bogey coming from above followed by another two, and from below another pair of bogies.

"Taking Pelican in a power descent have multiple bogies jumping me," Carol stated, hoping for help. She looked over at the spiders working feverishly on Danny. She wiped the sweat off her other palm and grabbed the stick with two hands. Quietly at first then louder, a voice came through a spider tapping rapidly on her ear. The voice came through a little soft at first, unbelievable but louder and surer, repeating, "Belay order, gladiators coming in from scramjet speed, high altitude bogeys are friendlies. Repeat high altitude bogeys are friendly."

Carol's vision became blurred as she almost passed out; the spiders put a mask on her as fumes filled the bridge. She pressed on. "I have multiple cascading problems with at least one medical emergency," she stated as calmly as she could. "Cargo one, what is your status? I cannot read telemetry."

Jets of carbon dioxide suppressed the fire, the emergency fire doors were closed, and emergency lighting flickered as the three started to move and retracted their restraints and head gear.

"Banged up a bit, nothing feeling too serious, how about you Jo?" Kali reported and queried.

"Same here," Jo answered; she unzipped the front of her life suit. Half-way down the child's head popped out.

"A boo," she said with a shy giggle, smiling face and happy like it was just a long game of peek-a-boo.

Joanne came back with a smiling, "A boo."

"This is Wren in Nexus 1. I have a trouble shooter drone and a pair of Gladiator class mantis coming to assist. Hold on sister we going to get this worked out." As the mantis drones passed the ship Carol looked out at them. 'Those are some chilling looking company,' Carol thought. As the second mantis passed it gave a slight nod. That's right, her thoughts were tied in to the network. The mantis took the comment as a compliment. The diagnostic drone hooked up to the plug INS on the exterior of the ship and sent the information to Wren. Because of the damage ship transmission was unavailable. The drone was working slavishly, getting as much straightened out as it could. Wren poured over the numbers and wondered what was really keeping this bird up. The distant percussion of the obliteration of the ships pursuing Carol was a welcome feeling.

The mantis ships came alongside the cockpit, one looked her way and tried to smile like a mantis mugging for a picture. It was just a shit eating grin. She heard Wren again.

"The two gladiators will wing tip you for stability until you come to the dome at the rally point. They don't have the opening for you to come through together with the guide drones, so you will have to land the ship with the repair drone helping to land the ship. Carol, this will not be easy. Use the interface on the stick to merge with the ship. Just think 'interface' when you grab a hold of the stick and it will tie in." Carol grabbed the stick and thought the word 'interface.' The merge pin jutted into the lower palm. The information action was locked in through Carol's nerves system to the ship's navigation network.

The time sped by. She saw the dome ahead. It was filling in getting ready to depart. "Carol, you have the ball, make the call," Wren instructed.

"Have night light visual on runway, gladiator break away in seven six, five, four, three, two, break..." The stick pulled hard. Carol's other hand wrapped the hand as her joints got yanked. She cleared the dome and dropped the ship quickly on approach. Joanne had her and the child secured in the cargo hold. The belts were tested as Carol did her best to keep the ship steady. The structure of the ship began to fail the closer she got to the runway. The landing gear folded as soon as they touched the ground. Carol reversed. Thrust fissures opened up in the ship now grinding on the tarmac. The fire crew blew foam on the smoldering ship. A cam mantis pulled the cargo door off as another gained entry to the cockpit.

Carol was led out coughing, Danny was on a stretcher being wheeled out, Kali and the child walked over to the stretcher. She handed off the child to a paramedic, asking, "Can you check her out?"

The triage doctor came over by Danny. "We need whole blood here!" he announced. Kali grabbed the stretcher. Her life suit set the direct transfusion as the spiders actively worked the tubing from the suit. "We need another stretcher here!" the doctor called as he steadied Joanne.

"Daddy!" Kali tearfully hugged him. He was alive, and Kali just knew that it was him. Danny's eyes opened; his only response was the trail of tears that rolled down his temples. Carol was so drained, her eyes so tired, she walked about twenty feet and then just sat down. The paramedic checked the child and she was just a bit bruised so she was sent on her way. She grabbed a few waters and an ice pack and walked over to Carol.

Resting the ice pack on her shoulder and handing her water the child spoke. "Diane." She rocked her body toward Carol. She was affixed. "Diane is my name. They said we should go to hangar fourteen." Diane pulled up on Carol's elbow. She instinctively got up and walked alongside the child to hangar fourteen. The strum of the guitar was faint, but somehow it picked a string of the heart that had a secure memory. It was a song by White Lion, 'When Children Cry.' It was sung as a lullaby. Carol remembered her mother singing it. Carol sang, choking off tears; she lifted Diane to her shoulder. Diane then sang as they stopped walking.

Carol saw things as getting so much better. Hearing this song just made her understand that whatever happened now they were free to carve their own destiny. Several people came from the hangar sensing the overwhelming emotion in the network.

Then there was a swooning shift and all became dark. The two masses from either side of the Earth coalesced and within a dark energy grid to form the small planetoid Ark that will be a vehicle to the New World, the lions portion of the planet will react with the dark energy core in an anti-matter reaction and fuel the needs of its citizens to seek a new home and destroy their enemies. The shuddering soon stopped with a strange new view: it was of galaxies flipping by like you were on a super celestial skyway, and the awareness of motion like one was on a commercial jetliner.

Wren and Kali stood above Lori lying in hospital bed. The operation, like all wars, had its causalities, and the old hospital was quite busy. The only change is that it was more of a nanoplex. The spiders were running the show. Military nurses and doctor were astounded at the rate of healing, their combined knowledge and experience with the spider proved miraculous. Lori's condition was a bit different. Lori ship's AI was stored in Lori with everything else that could be uploaded from ship before its destruction. She was cut off from the spider network by her own spiders concerned about a corruption, so until diagnosis was complete and repair paths taken she would be segregated from the network, but that did not mean Lori was stuck in bed.

Lori's eyes opened. She immediately realized from her vision that she was sharing her senses. Since the AI couldn't connect to the network it connected to her senses. Her vision came and went like two kids trying to share a pair of binoculars at a circus. Settling on one eye, each with a shared combined vision, which did get some getting used to as Lori sat up in bed, Wren adjusting the bed as she realized what Lori was trying to do.

Fourteen

❧ THE CHALLENGE ❧

*But the day of the Lord will come as a thief in the night, in which
the heavens will pass away with a great noise, and the elements
shall melt with a fervent heat, the Earth also and the works that
are therein shall be burned up. 2 Peter 3-10*

W ren, Kali and Naomi helped Lori up out of the bed.
"What!" Lori spoke out loud as the situation was
revealed to her. The military is about to hijack the
civil movement on the orders of Lt. Major Abrams. The plan had
worked to this point all that could be saved was saved in a
planetoid mass coalescing in a worm hole traveling to their New
World. The other half of the plan opened a worm hole next to a
rotating neutron star, a pulsar. The wormhole guided the deadly
gamma radiation to the other end of the worm hole right in the
path of the Troyon home world, which quickly voided it of all
life. The remaining military entered the relocation worm hole
not far behind them before the entrance closed, but Lori was the
Sextant and even though she was laid up they had no right for a
coup.

The quartet stood by the locked door of the military council, the locked doors hinges and locks fizzed in obliteration as Lori directed her spider's plasma web. Upon entering all stopped as Lori's spider jumped on the table and shot pins, anchoring Lt. Major Abrams to his chair, which began foaming, revealing his Troyon hybrid self.

"I am in charge here!" Lori's voice rang true and sure and sound. "This is why I am wary of your military. The spider is needed because there are Troyon vermin to be destroyed." Lori threw her hand toward the Troyon, who was slowing dissolving. Her eyes grabbed Carol's eyes as four other on the military council eyes just widened. "The rest here have been cleared and wear the spider, but I am too close to winning to allow you to have a Troyon soft hearted approach now."

"Winning, you don't know anything!" The Troyon spy spoke, beginning to screech, the plasma destroying the Troyon DNA, untying his life at a cellular level.

"I've had enough of you!" Lori's dagger unsheathed and slashed off the lower jaw of the spy. A gurgling mass of dying Troyon spilled to its destruction. There was a skipping in the air as a kind of deceleration took place.

"We're here!" Wren simply stated as the four took off, running to the control node. Upon entering Wren rushed into her nexus as Lori stood giving the command station staff orders.

"Bring outside visuals to screen. Let's see what is going on out there," Lori directed. "Wren, what is our power status?"

"We have power still flowing through worm hole, fully powered and operational. Kayla and her team establishing alternate power, to reestablish power after wormhole closure," Wren relayed to Lori.

Several military battle vessels emerged from the worm hole; the Troyon profile of pirated vessels gave Lori an aggressive demeanor. "Wren whatever you got that's operational and loaded I need in the air for a frontal defense. What is status of additional gravity because of us in this system? Is there a negative effect on our new home?"

"The massive ring system of outer planet is negating effects of added gravity added to system. We are good," Wren assured.

"Open me a channel to the approaching ships." Lori ordered. She saw the two snake fighters come screaming out of the wormhole. "Advancing military ships, cease approach until clear or you will be fired on! Wren, get me connected to a secure link to those snake fighters." Kali stood next to Lori, she had a trust in her since the battle and figured that was her place. She saw firsthand why there was this skepticism with the military, and how the Troyon had used it against them.

"I'm going outside to get my sisters together on this. We still have a lot of magic as a second wave if need be," Naomi said. Lori nodded and Naomi was off.

"I have a confirmed cloaked uncle transmission from the two snake fighters. 'Alive and well, possible internal threat advise caution.' Transmission ends there," Wren relayed. The ships stopped, but some seemed to take an attack posture, drifting into a flanking stance.

"Okay, Wren get everything we got in ready one for space assault, get the turrets up for battle. Don't like this here and don't want to be caught flatfooted," Lori stated as everyone quickly went to battle stations. The ready one flight wing was already on Lori's first thought.

"Military Armada you will not be able to merge with your civilian arm unless you comply one hundred percent with spider relationship. The web is stirring, alerting us to a threat of at least a dozen so please separate your self from this twelve," Lori stated. Wren then relayed a message to Lori. "I have quiet rumblings that the twelve are jamming the web communications hoping we fire on so the auto-defense system takes over. They are loading Atom poppers three rockets in salvos because we have gone to ready one."

"Fuck this nonsense," Lori said, just pissed. "We move forward. Kayla ready a full scouting party and the energy exchange cargo for the new home world. Wren, divert all fighters to escort scouting party and take defensive stature at planet. Evacuate whoever you can until I crack this stalemate."

"Confirm that Lori," Wren said. "I have reports of in fighting in military Armada."

"No Troyon shall pass me alive," Lori said with conviction.

"Military one to civilian one rescan we have neutralized threat." The military Armada reported. Lori thought then spoke.

"Puddles of plasma only option."

Lori looked out and saw the New World, and it was time to explore: a new day was dawning; it was time to find Sam and live life.

"Twelve puddles, confirm that Sextant." The Armada replied.

Fifteen

Do not let spacious plans for a new world divert your energies
from saving what is left by the old. Winston Churchill

The military waited for the civilian population to land and
off load before they landed. Lori, Scarlet and Hermes
stood in wait as a long-awaited reunion. The bay doors of
the flagship shuttle opened. Thirty armed soldiers hustled off
the shuttle and formed a perimeter, a bald Carmel skinned man
with a metal weighed uniformed walked out toward the three
who had gotten closer. Lori and the man extended their hands
for a handshake and introduction.

"General Matt Zenon and you must be?" He said looking at
Lori.

"I am Lori and this is Scarlet and Hemes Scarlet's Bodyguard
and consul." Matt shook Scarlet's hand, a low growl can from
Hermes he didn't extend his hand.

"Please excuse him he didn't have his breakfast this morning
he's a bit moody, he really doesn't like meeting new people."
Scarlet said taking a pouch from her belt approaching the General

and handing him the bag. "This contains seven tridents from seven of your warriors used as a key for a mission, I return them to you so they have a rightful place." Scarlet bowed her head and took a step back.

"Thank you for keeping them secure." Matt said. "Lori you and I must sit at the table of ideas and map out our next move." Lori simply nodded.

Matt and Lori sat next to each other a large desk in front of them with New World goals and timetables.

"Well Lori I think we should have a full response force we still don't know what all the repercussions may be." Matt said.

"Yes, but for you to learn our ways and us to learn yours it would be better to be joined in society. It is all our fight but we need a bit to get our footing here. We will have a response unit but we should activate in levels." Lori spoke thinking out a strategy. "A president Harry Truman once said, 'We must build a new world, a far better world-one in which the eternal dignity of man is respected.'" Matt downed the last of his drink and said.

"Let's just not forget who we are and where we come from." They both nodded in agreement. Mankind quickly grew into his new home as eight months passed quickly everything seemed to be on track.

Jake, Simon and Wendy walked along the tree line. The common thread that sowed these three together was that they identified themselves as explores. Jake the more vocal and Simon was sensitive with quiet intelligence, Wendy rounded out the three as their intermediary of both their ideas, being the oldest and a blonde pony tailed tomboy.

"Yes but I saw it, it was some sort of platform I studied the aerial reconnaissance." Simon stated. Jake's head rolled with his eyes.

"Yeah well you better be right about this. This platform is far we'll need transportation." Jake looked at Wendy with another head rolling jester and said. "So Wendy, you do know this witch Scarlet and she's just going to let us use her Blue Heron Broom to check out this shadow of Simons'. That's hard to believe."

As Jake shifted his field of vision left, at eye level he saw a pair of short ankle cut Victorian Boots with buckles and silver decorated heel spikes, Jake looked up higher following the legs to Scarlet sitting side saddle on her Blue Heron broom looking down on him.

"Those are some righteous boots Scarlet!" Wendy said. Scarlet slowed and lowered down as she kicked off her broom and stood next to them.

"Thanks, yes the boots I found them I think there were witches in this forest long ago." Scarlet stated. "Well I don't think the broom can fly all of us around but I did find something else we may be able to use." Scarlet pointed to two fir trees a little bit ahead of them. "Head over to those two trees and go between them I have something to show you." Simon froze, Scarlet walked over to him and quietly asked. "What do you see Simon?"

"Before my alarm woke me this morning I had a dream." Simon explained. "I didn't even remember it until now, kind of a déjà vu. A weathered gray bearded man introduced himself to me as John Muir, I could tell he loved the land. Well he and I were walking through a forest like this one and he pointed to two fir trees just like the ones you pointed to and he said.

"Between every two pine trees there is a door leading to a new way of life."

"Well that clinches it for me. Simon says we go!" Jake said boldly taking lead and walking to the trees.

Thirty yards inside from the gateway pines was a simple hole in the ground looking in just seemed like a ten foot drop to the bottom? Scarlet took a small rock and dropped it in the hole where it quickly disappeared. Without a word she held her broom and walked into the hole and disappeared. The three followed. Scarlet stood her halo aglow with enough light to see a Labyrinth of gears, leavers and valves, she spun one valve and the light grew around them she began to walk the three closely in tow. Scarlet reaching the proper door turned large bulkhead knobs and pulled door shanks across, and opened the door to.

"An airship!" Jake eyes wide open. A five person enclosed bridge supported by a large football shaped ballast made of alloy metals with the shine of fresh struck copper. They all walked around in awe as Scarlet then spoke.

"I like to tinker with things finding this place was like finding my own workshop. I have been in contact with a few of the engineers and they tell me the physics of fire and water is different here. The firebox is small, so is the water tank but in this realm a little goes a long way is safe to say. So what say you three, I need a flight crew." The new explores were ecstatic. Scarlet instructed them to collect dry wood from the forest and fresh water from a close by stream, upon returning Scarlet passed out worn personal protection equipment steam goggles, leather looking fire resistant gloves and aprons. Scarlet explained their duties inside Jake stoke the firebox, Simon on steam control and Wendy navigation and pilot the ship. Scarlet would be the Captain because it was her ship.

"All set then let's go." Scarlet proclaimed. The three all feeling a bit rushed and tired.

"Well can we come back tomorrow and start this." Simon said with a yawn.

"No, not really I put a spider block in place so no one would know what we are doing or worry about us but, don't know how long it will last couple days maybe." Scarlet said. "Okay I will go and get some provisions and we will leave at daybreak. The three of you can stay the night."

"What about drinking water?" Jake asked.

"You can drink the water from the stream its fine I drink it all the time." Scarlet stated. The three children eyes all met, as they turned back to Scarlet to give her a rebuttal she was gone. They drank the rest of the water they had brought with, if need be they would drink the stream water in the morning, the day's toil helped close their eyes.

Wendy awoke a little startled she thought she heard something. Then she heard it again, awake, it was the chattering of a cat. It was cat talking, Wendy followed her ears to the corridor, she heard it again and as she looked in that direction she saw a cat scurry over to a door and vanish in a shadow. A blue glowing ball about the size of a ping pong ball quickly flew into the room. Wendy knew she just had to follow.

Rocket hovered by the dressing table rummaging through a few jewelry boxes. Wendy's eyes rounded the corner and a strange cat vocalization rang out. "Come over here Wendy I want to share something with you." Rocket said. "My name is Rocket by the way." Wendy walked over to her. "I have been following Scarlet it seems as though she has been blocking the spider tracking. Well as I was following her wind spirits from this planet brought a voice to me of a girl who once lived here, in fact this was her room and that airship was her father's."

"Is this girl angry with us?" Wendy asked.

"No, on the contrary she is very sweet and understanding and she has gifts for us." Rocket said with a smile. "That closet there in the corner has airship crew cloths and riggings a regular haberdashery. Her father and brothers used it as their ready room. She says the boys need to dress proper." Wendy began looking through the jewelry boxes as Rocket yelled out. "This is it!" She laid it down in front of Wendy to show her. It was a heart shaped locket but the outside looked like the fire box door in the airship it had venting grid and a gear latch and was colored by fire seasoning. Rocket opened it and it read. 'Your fire keeps our steamy love alive'. "He will just love this!" Rocket said. "Anything tickles your fancy Wendy?"

Wendy's hand reached deep down into the box as she pull out a copper and brass wrist cuff ornately twisted copper set on a brass chain connected to a amethyst dragon eye ring, it seemed to fit perfect. "Yes I like this." Wendy said, admiring its look on her arm.

Rocket was so quiet of wing she just hovered by Wendy's ear and spoke so softly. "This meeting must all be kept secret you never saw me. If anyone asks you, you found these things looking for a cat you heard. I have one more thing to give you." It felt like a feather touch so soft on Wendy's neck and she turned to see Rocket fly across the room she scampered over to her as she stopped by a small door in the wall, a safe but with only a single lever. "I need help with this lever Twitch and I couldn't get it open." Wendy went and pulled on it with her arm without her new jewelry and the lever seemed stuck, but when she used her cuff clad arm the lever opened as if it were freshly oiled. Wendy pulled out a metal box and opened it, inside was a metal sphere a little smaller than a baseball. "Scarlet will come tomorrow and get the fire and water going and energy levels will be up but the ship will not lift. Scarlet has tried several times. This time you have a key and you must find where it goes."

"What are you up to?!" Simon's voice broke the air. Wendy looked around and Rocket wasn't to be seen.

"Heard a cat, then I stumbled upon this room." Wendy simply stated placing the orb in a small shoulder shackle that was inside the box.

"A cat I haven't heard any cat. Who were you talking to?" Simon questioned.

"I was calling to the cat." Wendy said. Just then Twitch ran so quickly out the door startling Simon. "See" she said. "I have some things to show you." Wendy and Simon started looking through the clothes in the closet.

First light arrived and so did Scarlet. Standing next to the airship was the three crew members all decked out in their airship wardrobe. "Now there we go that's the spirit." Scarlet seemed so pleased the trio was more motivated than the night before. "Boys topside and bring down the supplies fill the water containers and Wendy and I will plot a course." Scarlet ordered her crew.

The boys were off double quick. "I have something I found for you." Wendy said leading Scarlet to the girl's room and showing her a black lacey bombardier dress with an open front and full back skirt. The accompanying blouse front had laces with red piping. "I thought these would match those shoes perfectly."

"Stars and broomsticks that dress and shoes are just a perfect match." Scarlet said holding the dress admiring it. Wendy helped her put the dress on right over her life suit.

Together at the airship they looked like the regular crew from years ago. Jake got that fire right up and Simon regulated the boilers, the wood burnt and kept fire like the darkest coal without any noxious fumes. Once the furnace got hot steam power started to flow, Scarlet went to the control wall and hit the switches to direct steam to the three axis gyroscope navigation system. The ship hummed from gyros. "Well crew that's about as far as I ever get we should take off now but nothing." Scarlet shifting her lips trying to figure her next move. Wendy walked up to her and reached down in that bag and took that sphere out and showed it to Scarlet.

"If this were a key for the craft where would it be?" Wendy asked.

"The main control panel." Scarlet stated grabbing Wendy's arm and pulling her to the panel. They looked and saw nothing that matched the sphere. Then Wendy saw the one empty panel had a strange indentation. She took the sphere in her hand and twisted it in her fingers the center stretched out from between the two ends and fit the inlay on the panel. A long horn sounded as gears spun outside lifting the pistons that opened the bay door above. Wendy went to the pilot chair and steadied the big wheel as she eased on the power petals the ship began to rise up, higher past the tree tops, everyone was all smiles.

Then a red light started to flash on the console and a buzzer started pulsing, two gauges pinned themselves in the red. "Soot pipe is blocked." Scarlet announced. "Open the blowout valve Simon." Simon spun and opened valve fourteen, not being that familiar with the craft he neglected to close the draft. The soot not only blew out the outside stack but filled the cabin with black hot soot. Scarlet made her way to the panel and vented the cabin, other than soot film all over, some coughing and blotches of black soot on the crew all was fine.

"Guess that's why we have all this protection gear on." Scarlet stated.

"Scarlet we are gaining altitude fast." Wendy announced.

"Simon divert steam to navigation control, valve twelve open full." Scarlet ordered. Wendy felt the life come into rudders and flaps. "Wendy set course to vector 117, half steam." Scarlet said Wendy and Simon quickly complied. Jake fed the firebox.

"Okay all hate to ask a question but, how do we know where to go, we're in a ship with several small glass portals around a witch with a broom who's never seen the maps Simon has, kind of lost before we really get started." Jake stated.

"Oh you all are going to love this feature!" Scarlet said catching her breath as she spun several wheel knobs on the control panel. The floor became transparent they all had an aerial view. "A set of lenses under the bridge projects a real time picture to the viewer which in this case is the entire floor. Wendy saw Simon's quick breath, his eyes darting across the topography in a crazed fashion.

"Wendy!" Simon said loudly. "Can you come about around that set of large trees? Once I verify our position looks like we will be heading into the rising Sun." Wendy maneuvered the ship around the trees. Simon nodded his head. "Head directly into the Sun I should have another visual guidepost in about ten minutes at this speed." Simon stepped over to the steam wall and put a new head of steam on as the steam turbine spun faster.

Scarlet stayed in the ship with the three she really didn't want to be alone on her broom. She enjoyed the company. The Sun was touching the horizon in back of them when Simon proclaimed. "Visual verification of platform, Wendy easy turn left do you see it?" They all saw it.

"Jake bank the fire. Simon vent steam to exterior. Wendy put her down right in that clearing in the center. Simon vent steam to the electric generator, twilight is on us." Scarlet ordered. The ship landed with a light tinny bump. "Okay we go outside no further than thirty yards around the ship stay in the light we are not equipped for night exploration we will set out at daybreak." The two moons showing themselves in the dimming sky, and the crew checking the exterior of an airship, this was their new world and a new way of life.

The first rays of morning light diffused off the horizon slowly bringing the ambient light levels higher. Jake reached in his pocket and took out a small book and pencil.

'Many bird species on this planet just as noisy as birds back on Earth were on those early summer mornings. I should start to draw some of them they are beautiful. We made it to the platform today need to take a look about. It's very peaceful here-serene.'

"Ready Jake?" Simon asked. Jake got up pocketed his notebook and the four started walking around the platform. Through the center of a clearing they saw a set of train tracks that were unseen at a distance, but up close the tracks were visible. The platforms were areas for people to load onto trains but, hadn't seen a train yet, or another person.

"We have several building here let's get a look inside." Wendy directed. The four walked into one building there were stairs and smoke box display. Surrounded by hangings on the walls were pictures of people during the construction of the platform. Wendy was attracted to one picture of a boy with his father standing on the stairs of a train engine.

"Find something interesting Wendy?" Scarlet asked.

"Just trying to imagine being here when these photos were taken is all." Wendy answered. They walked around taking in the sights of the area, Scarlet was walking around outside looking at the mounted time pieces as Wendy, Simon and Jake headed to the steam generator building.

Rocket hovered by Hector her flittering was a tell that she had something brewing. "What do you got there little one?" Hector asked, as Rocket unfolded a cloth containing the locket she found.

"Well," Rocket started getting her thoughts together. "Ever since we met it seems we have some sort of connection, I feel so close to you."

"And I you Rocket, I believe it is because of my wings, I love to fly and since you're the embodiment of the air spirit we have a connection. Hector said trying to explain his soulful longing to be with Rocket. Rocket stood in Hectors palm and showed him the locket.

"I have this gift for you, because no matter why, I love you." Rocket confessed. Hector heart burned with affection as she read the inscription to him. Hector had never been given a gift because of love before, it was hard for Hector to keep down his growing emotions. "I think our spirits were close at the creation of the universe that why I feel so comfortable with you. I have a perfect place for the locket if I may?" Rocket asked. Hector nodded afraid to speak because his voice would crack in emotion. Rocket flew to Hector's breast plate and took the locket pushing it up under a scale right over one his hearts. As Rocket flew and kissed his cheek, Hector spoke out loud as Hermes communicated with him.

"Yes Hermes I will go and find her now! Rocket seems as though Scarlet is missing and a block has been put up to hide her, I have orders to find her, I must leave."

"I saw them this morning, I can take you there it's not too far. That is if you can keep up!" Rocket said with a playful tone and was gone. Hector smiled to himself and followed her slip stream.

Large blue pipes lead to a steam turbine electric generator, after exploring a bit they ended up by a control panel with valves and different sized pipes leading in and out with gauges and leavers. Wendy stood next to Jake close to the board Simon stood back a bit studying the panel. Jake looked over to Wendy and winked.

"I wonder what this valve is for?" Jake said setting up his prank. He acted like he turned the valve and with his mouth made a steam hissing sound with his back to Simon.

"O my Jake what valve did you touch the system is still energized we must tell Scarlet." Simon said quickly.

"No Simon don't bother it is just a joke." Jake relayed.

"This is no joke," Simon countered. "This must be fixed, it's dangerous." Simon turned and hurried out Jake and Wendy right behind him. Jake went to a swipe at Simon to stop him and explain. Jake unknowing and in the heat of the moment all went unnoticed, that Jake knocked some nano mites off of Simon's clothes. They were inactive Simon carried them just to have them if needed. As the three ran and the nanos hit the floor the devices went into probe mode. First the nanos artificial intelligence realized it was no longer connected to the rest of the system. It began reviewing the last few minutes of recorded information before they were activated. They heard Simon say 'it must be fixed it' dangerous' and that the three fled quickly. The nanos crawled to the rays of light coming in and started using solar energy to multiply; they had a mission now, to fix the generator.

Simon ran up to Scarlet breathless and excited to explain what happened which Scarlet heard as gibberish. Jake kept saying and over. "It was just a joke." Edging the words in at Simon's breath stops. A warning horn sounded.

"That doesn't sound like a joke, everybody back to the ship." Scarlet ordered. The nanos had set off an internal alarm in the generator house. The four got into the ship Jake stoked the firebox and got the steam up quickly. The alarm from the generator stopped. Simon went to open the valves to start the gyroscopes but, none of the valves would open. They all tried, so did Wendy with her jewelry clad hand but to no avail. "Must be some kind of steam lock, Jake is so good at the firebox he brought the steam pressure up so fast it vapor locked the valves. Okay then lets vent all steam out Simon so we can reduce the pressure." Scarlet ordered thinking the problem through.

Just then there was a thunder pop as if lightning had struck right next to the ship. Scarlet eyes opened wide. I'll go outside to see what that was you three keep working on our flight prob-lems. Scarlet opened the door and slipped out, she looked from where the thunder pop came from.

"Your sister's aren't very happy with you." Hector said. Scarlet relieved, yet she knew she was in some deep dragon dung.

"Well, we'll be underway in a bit have a few things to iron out let my sister know you found me we'll be back by night fall." Scarlet said turning walking back to the ship, after she entered Hector picked up the ship and said.

"That's not how it works I have to bring you back so hang on I will fly you there. Shut down your furnace and vent your steam my scales can use a bit of a cleaning." Hector said as he took to the air. Standing there watching was Lilith with a puzzled expression, a scoffed breath of disbelief, and then she said ouloud.

"You cannot escape your destiny that easily. There is a dark moon rising."

ABOUT THE AUTHOR

Peter Hackiewicz was born September 27, 1960 in the Back of the Yards, Chicago, Illinois. He attended St. Augustine Grammar School and St. Joseph High School. He likes to write science-fiction and fantasy and has worked in a cemetery for thirty-six years married for twenty-eight years raising three girls. He is a resident of Illinois and lives in the south west suburbs. Pete writes when he can and as his children get older he is dedicating time to his writing and believes he has something that you would be interested in reading. You can visit his website at www.sororityoftheninthfold.com.

www.ingramcontent.com/pod-product-compliance
Lightning Source LLC
Chambersburg PA
CBHW071522170626
46811CB00007B/2926